What the c[...]

"UNCHARTERED WATERS is an exciting and sassy pleasure from start to finish. New author Jodi Lynn Copeland writes a sizzling tale that makes hearts pound furiously and leaves readers breathless. Stephie and Nick are fascinating characters who were "bad" beneath the surface, just dying to come out and play." – *Tracey West, Road to Romance*

"I very much enjoyed these two characters who struggled for the right balance during their heated weekend. It is always a thrill for me to read debut authors. Ms. Copeland is no exception." – *Robin Taylor, In the Library Reviews*

"From start to finish this book is sure to hold your attention and soften the heart." – *Angel Brewer, The Romance Studio*

"UNCHARTED WATERS; is one of those novels that as you read you gain a bigger picture and there are parts of the tale that are very emotional. The characters are wonderful..." – *Gail Northman, Romance Junkies*

"UNCHARTED WATERS is both a fun and a serious story. Some of the scenes can be shocking, but enjoyable at the same time... If you are looking for a story that is both romantic and full of wild, steamy fun, check out UNCHARTED WATERS." – *Enya Adrian, Romance Reviews Today*

Uncharted Waters
An Ellora's Cave publication, 2003

Ellora's Cave Publishing, Inc.
PO Box 787
Hudson, OH 44236-0787

ISBN # 1843607492

ISBN MS Reader (LIT) ISBN # 1-84360-645-3
Other available formats (no ISBNs are assigned):
Adobe (PDF), Rocketbook (RB), Mobipocket (PRC) &
HTML

UNCHARTED WATERS edited by Pamela Campbell.
Cover art by Scott Carpenter.

UNCHARTED WATERS

Jodi Lynn Copeland

Chapter 1

"Waited too long!"

Stephanie Lang rehashed her boyfriend's, correction, her ex-boyfriend's words with her hands firmly curled around her BMW's steering wheel, lest they find their way back up to Greg Chisolm's apartment and around his no-good neck.

Waited too long, my ass. The only thing she had waited too long for was to figure out what a world-class jerk Greg was. She'd actually trusted him, believed she was in love with him. Enough to take the afternoon off work to voyage into previously uncharted waters. She'd spent two and a half hours in lingerie and fetish shops for him today. Endured personal embarrassment, not to mention spending most of her paycheck on gadgets that required detailed instructions to use, only to find him in bed with another woman.

"You waited too long, babe," he'd said with as much concern as a hawk right before it jammed its talons into a helpless little field mouse. "A guy can only go so long without sex."

Or what? He'd implode?

Whatever happened to the dickhead, she wasn't going to mourn the end of their relationship. She and Greg had been going out for six months, and she could just about guarantee he'd given up on her long before this. Especially if the way that hussy had her mouth wrapped around his penis was any sign.

She would have done that for him, if he'd only waited another couple hours.

Screw that, she was glad he hadn't waited, because then she would have gone on believing he gave a damn about her and her chest would hurt even more than it already did. That couldn't be heartache that pressed at her breastbone, definitely not tears threatening to burst free. *The man's a loser, Stephanie. Don't you dare cry over him!*

"Son of a bitch," she vented, as hot tears trickled down her cheeks. She wasn't going to mourn him! The man was a sleaze ball—unworthy of her love and sure as hell unworthy of her tears.

Squaring her shoulders, Stephanie sniffed back her emotions and jetted out of the parking lot of Greg's apartment complex. Her thoughts turned from the faithless idiot upstairs to her true agenda for this weekend—to finally satisfy her seven-year itch.

She'd planned to end her celibacy streak and give in to Greg's every fantasy during their two-day pleasure cruise on Lake Michigan. She'd been waiting for what seemed an eternity for Mr. Right to come along, or at least a Mr. Maybe she could trust enough to indulge her slightly unusual carnal demands. She thought she'd found that man in Greg.

Wrong!

Six lousy months down the tube and all she had to show for it was smeared mascara. Well, no more tears or wasted time. The wait was over.

Starting today, right this second, she was a woman on a mission. She was going to find Mr. Close Enough and get laid. In a way she wanted. In a way she deserved. In a way that would give her total and complete control, with no chance of emotions getting involved.

Love sucked, and she was through with it once and for all.

* * * * *

Long legs, a tight ass, and a rack any man would love to get his hands on.

Whoever the blonde strutting her way through the swarm of naked and barely dressed partiers was, she ought to know better than to come out to Murphy's Harbor without an escort. The secluded clothing-optional marina resort where Nick Calanetti worked weekends was crawling with men looking for a prime piece like her. Hell, maybe she was looking for the same thing.

Something told him that if she was, she was a long way out of her league. The confident walk and eat-'em-alive smile she'd put on the moment she'd stepped from her Beemer lacked a certain finesse, as if she'd only just decided to break them out. With her fire engine red mouth, too tight top, tiny shorts and high-heeled sandals streamlining her shapely tanned legs, she looked like a woman on the prowl.

Beyond that, Nick sensed another layer. There was something about being a nice guy in a resort full of bad boys—you could spot another nice guy from a hundred yards away. Even if that nice guy happened to be a woman.

Reaching the landing, the blonde swung the bloated duffel bag from her shoulder to the wood planks at her feet. She slipped off her dark sunglasses and started down the first dock to the *Hidden Desire's* slip. Her deep brown eyes honed in on Nick's face, drifted to the polished chrome side rail he leaned against, then back up again. Her smile blossomed into a grin that said she'd found what she was looking for and couldn't be happier.

"Nice," Drake Matson, Nick's long-time friend, remarked from where he sat drinking a beer and fighting off the sweltering July heat on the pleasure cruiser's cushioned bench seat.

"For a spoiled rotten daddy's girl," Nick agreed dryly, with a second glance at the shiny black Beemer from which she had emerged.

For all her God-given attributes, the woman didn't look a day over twenty-one. That kind of car took a hell of a lot more life experience to afford. Unless, of course, she had her daddy buy it for her. Or maybe her sugar daddy.

Drake smirked. "Whoever she is, I think she wants you." He tipped the beer bottle toward his mouth. "And I meant that exactly the way it sounded."

Nick let go an expected 'get real' laugh. He worked at the risqué resort on summer weekends as a way to escape his humdrum weekday life as a newspaper columnist and self-appointed guardian to his younger sister, Emily. While he'd be the first to say the scenery at Murphy's Harbor was a definite fringe benefit, out of respect for the employee/guest moderated fraternization rule he never sampled the fare.

He stuck to his job, carting couples out onto the water for a two-day getaway living out their most erotic fantasies. As the happy duo grunted and groaned, he worked on his columns in the privacy of his soundproof cabin and on his waterside deck. Along with adding some excitement to his life, the part-time job gave him the chance to escape the onshore summer heat, and this year, the relentless muggy nights.

Only he had a feeling about the woman on the dock. One that said the walls of his soundproof cabin wouldn't be enough to block out her grunts and groans. The gentle breeze that rolled off the lake sure wouldn't be enough to thwart the effect her curvaceous body had on his own. And that pretty much ruled out all chance of his nights being anything less than torridly hot.

Maybe she wasn't here for the purpose of renting the boat, maybe she was lost. Clinging to that hope, Nick swiveled.

The blonde stood a few feet away, her eyes wide and her shirt too damned impossibly tight and tiny for even a nice guy to ignore. A thin gold necklace dipped into the hollow where her plentiful cleavage pushed together, then disappeared out of sight. With all that natural padding, it'd take a man an awful long time to find out where the strand of gold ended.

He envisioned filling his hands with her lush breasts, drawing her peaked, burning nipples into his mouth and sucking at their distended, slippery tips until she revealed the secret of the lost strand and so much more.

Feeling his cock harden, he dragged his gaze back to her face. She stood, taking in the boat from bow to stern. She looked almost awestruck, her painted mouth drawn up in an 'O', that he couldn't help but notice with just a little effort would fit the male parts of his anatomy to perfection. His shaft thickened further with the thought of her velvety tongue sliding along its sensitive ridges, suckling the moisture from the swelled head, and leaving the cherry red imprint of her lips in her wake.

He shifted, attempting to ignore the surge of pheromones jetting through his bloodstream, making his shorts feel like they were made for someone half his size. Blondie might look like the kind of voluptuous siren wet dreams were based on, but instinct told him she was gentle as a kitten. Still, he couldn't help but wonder, if the outside of the cruiser made her so happy, how she would respond to the inside, and all the kinky toys the lower level had to offer. Would she purr, or run the other way?

He waited a beat, before asking, "You lost?"

"Not if this is the *Hidden Desire*."

Like her walk, her voice held confidence undercoated with uncertainty. Daddy's girl or not, her contrasts were intriguing. So was the rest of her barely clothed body.

"That's what it says on the hull," he said.

Setting her chin, she stepped closer. All trace of hesitance left her eyes as she swept her gaze the length of him. She lingered in the general direction of his groin, and his erection pressed harder against his shorts, bringing a silent curse to his lips.

An impish smile curved the corners of her mouth when she returned to his face. A smile that made Nick wonder if she could read his mind. Or worse, spot his all but erect cock beneath the thin shirt and shorts that covered it.

"Are you the captain of this boat?" she asked.

His senses went on full alert at the change in her tone. She no longer sounded soft or kittenish, but seductive and purposeful. Like she had every intention of renting the cruiser and fully enjoying its amenities.

Two days trapped on a boat with her and her lover, now didn't that sound like the last place on earth he wanted to be. His gut churned at the renewed thought of her pleasured groans cutting into the silence of his safe haven, groans elicited by another man. One who probably didn't know how lucky he was to have such a natural wonder as the honey standing before him. And she was natural. Plastic didn't look that good.

"I take it out on the water if that's what you mean," he clipped.

"Hmm...you don't say."

Her lips parted once more, this time to reveal dazzlingly white teeth. Her tongue darted out and ran over her full lower lip. She slowly retracted it, until nothing but the pink tip remained, then that too disappeared, leaving a shimmering wetness behind, and a savage throb in his shorts.

Nick bit back a groan. How the hell could he ever have thought her a nice girl? Nice girls didn't make secret promises via shoulda-been-innocent swipes of their tongues. And that's exactly what she'd just done. The twinkle in her eyes ensured she knew the effect she was having on him, the erotic images drifting through his mind—visions of hot, sweaty limbs and a pink, swollen pussy quivering for release.

Blondie wasn't a nice girl at all. She was bad to the bone. A sexual predator who knew how to search out and carnally manipulate her prey. He should be glad she had a partner to keep her busy, but for whatever reason the knowledge irritated him.

"You'll do nicely," she murmured.

Right, he would. And what exactly did she have in mind? If it involved another man, count him out. Scratch that, count him out anyway. Where the hell was his head? Oh yeah, lodged between his balls.

Nick struggled for casualness, while his body drew tauter with each passing second. "You looking to reserve a weekend?"

"I'm looking to take a cruise, a pleasure cruise." She drawled out the word pleasure then added with a slow wink, "Today. With you."

"Sorry, we're booked."

"I know," she purred. "For two long, steamy nights."

She leaned so close he couldn't stop from zeroing in on the top of her plump, tanned breasts pushing against her shirt. They wanted to get out. He hoped to God she didn't let them. So much as a nipple showed itself and he was liable to do something really stupid, like snag himself a mouthful.

Her words sank in then and he jerked his gaze to her face. Holy shit, this was his weekend party? Trouble in a tiny T-shirt and where the hell was her partner?

She extended a slender hand, adorned with the kind of fuck-me red nails that were made for digging into a man's back. Kitten he'd guessed. More like a tiger fresh to the hunt. And if he was reading her right, he was her mark of the day.

"Stephie Lang," she offered, "and you're…?"

In serious trouble. "Your reservation's under two names."

Her red-hot lips formed a knowing smile. "Greg won't be able to make it."

Ah, Christ. "So, it's just you?"

Her smile edged higher. "And you."

Right. Greg's replacement. That was going to happen. Like never.

"I don't think you understand how this operation works," Nick said, doing his best to keep the internal struggle of body over mind from his voice. If he let his body call the shots and they'd be putting the lower level to use before they left shore. "I take you out on the water, get you acquainted with the equipment then magically disappear for two days while you and your lover realize every sexual fantasy you've ever had."

A flush of crimson sprang into Stephie's cheeks. "It doesn't have to go that way though, right?" she asked, her voice low and husky, ensuring the color in her face wasn't from embarrassment but something else entirely. "I mean, you could stay around if you wanted to, right?"

"I don't actually go anywhere, I just stay in my cabin."

Her eyes sparkling with excitement, she leaned over the side rail, and set her long nails on his bared forearm, tracing the bunched muscle upward and shooting ten-hundred watts of raw desire straight to his drawn balls.

"So, if I get bored, I can come visit you in your cabin?"

Nick jerked his arm away. He was willing to play the dock boy in need of a stroke for a minute or two, but definitely not the entire weekend. Nice guys liked hot sex as much as bad boys. They might even fantasize about doing it with complete strangers. But as he routinely pointed out to Emily, they didn't go through with the act. More importantly, nice guys didn't break company rules that could lead to their termination.

He crossed his arms over his chest and narrowed his gaze. "Look, you wanna go out on the water alone for the weekend, that's your call. Just don't expect me to supply the entertainment."

"Aye, aye, captain." Stephie gave a mock salute and started toward the shore.

He watched her go, his gaze constant on her curvy ass. The swell of her naked butt cheeks peeked beneath the frayed hem of her jean shorts with each of her steps and took away any hope his cock had of going limp in the next hour or so.

He breathed a sigh of relief when she reached the end of the dock. She was leaving. As much as he might be tempted to take her up on all she had to offer and bury his face in the softness of her ripe breasts, he knew he'd only regret it in the long run. He already had way too much on his mind to have to deal with remorse too.

Nick's relief died a frustrated death when Stephie hefted the duffel bag over her shoulder a moment later and retraced her steps to the side of the boat. Her smile huge and her deep brown eyes full of promise, she asked in a smoky tone, "So, what do you say I board now, captain? I'm way overdue for a pleasure cruise."

* * * * *

Stephanie took in the cruiser's cabin, more than a little happy she'd decided to stick with her weekend plans aboard the *Hidden Desire*. Given the boat was docked at Murphy's Harbor, she figured finding a prime stud willing to meet her sexual demands would be easy. When she saw the dazzling duo on the *Hidden Desire* itself, her plan switched from snagging a resort guest to bagging a resort employee.

Both men were tall and built, but the one with the sin-black hair and sea green eyes had a sexual pull too potent to ignore.

Speaking of sin-black, the enormous cruiser's cabin was canvassed in the shade. Several windows lined the seating area walls, but they were swathed in black velvet drapes. The bountiful bedroom had no windows at all. What it lacked in windows though, it more than made up for in playthings.

She'd seen dildos before, had a couple of her own at home and a brand new vibrating one in her bag along with a handful of other goodies. Still, as she took in the menagerie of plastic gizmos and metal thingies, she realized her sexual knowledge was sadly lacking.

Not that she hadn't known that.

Aside from the occasional orgasm she supplied herself, her sexual experience was limited to one painful event she'd just as soon forget.

There would never be a repeat of that time. She hadn't put off sex as long as she had for nothing. She was smarter now, older. At twenty-six she had more than a great paying, though boring job, as a financial analyst for Gamble & Net. She had security and a sense of self. She knew what she wanted and, thanks to that two-timing dickhead's eye opener, she knew that something wasn't love. It was sex. Pure and simple sexual gratification. And she planned to get it. Soon.

She could have picked an easier target.

Not that the green-eyed Adonis upstairs wasn't attracted to her. A moron couldn't have missed the way his shirt tented out in the front. The longer she stood there talking, the more his shirt edged toward her, until she wondered how big he was going to grow. For a second she considered not stroking his arm at all but going right for the object of her attention, and filling her hand up with inch after inch of prime male flesh. Only they'd had company.

And frankly, she wasn't that gutsy.

Correction, the old Stephanie wasn't that gutsy. The new Stephie was more daring than a tightrope walker without a net. The new Stephie acknowledged the way the Adonis upstairs had stared at her chest, like he was starving for a bite of what she had beneath her shirt. The new Stephie reveled in his attention and the wetness that seeped though her bikini bottom when she thought about taking his penis into her mouth the way that hussy had been doing to Greg when she walked in on them.

She'd take him in, until his erection tickled her tonsils, and then she'd taste him. Suck on him, run her tongue over every glorious inch of his masculinity, until his musky scent filled her nose and his come filled her throat.

And the Adonis would let her. Once she had him handcuffed to the bed, he wouldn't have much of a choice.

More than ready to get this weekend rolling, Stephanie slipped off her shirt and shorts to reveal the string bikini beneath. She ought to start right out bare-chested. Maybe bare-assed too. She would, if not for the way the stranger had acted when he realized it would just be the two of them this weekend. His hard-on hadn't faded any, but he hadn't looked too pleased either.

She'd take her clothes off soon enough, but first she had to learn his name—and his fantasies. Her notion of love might be jaded, but she still believed in mutual satisfaction. She wouldn't be the only one getting off from their encounter.

Stephanie moved into the unsurprisingly black bathroom and stared in awe at the hundred or more bottles of body sprays, lotions and oils before her. They lined two rows of a four-foot long shelf and sported wrappers that boasted flavors from chocolate to tequila sunrise.

They'd have to sample each flavor, she thought with a smile. One lick at a time.

Turning away from the shelf, she caught her reflection in the mirror and her smile widened. In the winter she always felt too pale, but in the summer, once she got a good tan, she was confident with her looks, knew the large breasts she'd bemoaned in her early teens were now an aphrodisiacal magnet that attracted a man's eye like a bee to honey. The man upstairs being no exception.

She dashed a spray of cinnamon spritzer over her body, then removed her necklace and laid it on the sink basin. Her grandmother had given her the cross necklace for her sixteenth birthday, and normally she never took it off. But something told her finding a cross hanging between her boobs would be more than enough of a buzz kill to halt any progress she made with the sexy stranger.

She didn't want a buzz kill. She didn't want anything to keep her away from his pleasurable looking mouth and the hard lean lines of his body. Her Adonis was built to suit, and the day's growth of dark scruff on his tanned face would be more than a little appealing brushing up against her naked, sweaty flesh.

A jolt of excitement dashed along her spine, tightening her nipples and curling warmth low in her stomach. Soon she would feel his mouth on her breasts, and kissing her between her thighs, right along with the flick of his tongue over her clit, making her arch up and beg for more.

For the second time in the last hour, wetness pooled between her legs coloring the air with her own heady scent. She welcomed it with a giddy smile as she pirouetted out of the bathroom and toward the front of the massive cabin.

Good-bye Stephanie Lang good girl—hello Stephie Lang, bad girl on a mission. She was going to spend this weekend indulging her every fantasy. And Mr. Close Enough was going to love every minute of it, even if she had to strap him down to get him to give in. And she would strap him down. Ankle and wrist cuffs were a necessity to maintain control. They were also a luxury she'd enjoy using to the fullest extent.

Chapter 2

Nick scrubbed a hand over his face and sank down on the seat kiddy corner from Drake. The next two days were going to be the hardest of his life, for every part of his body. Resisting Stephie's advances when another man was in tow was one thing. Resisting them when it was just the two of them, alone on a forty-foot pleasure cruiser that was decked to the gills with sex toys, would be damned near impossible.

"I don't suppose you'd be interested in spending the weekend on the lake?" he asked Drake, only half joking.

His friend raised a russet eyebrow. "Don't tell me she scares you, man."

"Not even close." What she did was worry him. Shook up his resolve to stick to company rules and not mix business with pleasure. Not to mention prove every word he'd told his sister about nice guys not sleeping with strangers false.

He'd been attracted to plenty of strangers, physically turned on by more than a few. He'd never considered sticking his cock in a single one of them. All right, he had considered it. But he'd never done anything beyond considering. Never taken action on the idea the way Stephie had him wanting to do.

"As much as I'd love to help you, Nick—and trust me I would—I have a date with Alexis tonight. You know I can't say no to her."

Nick's worries were temporarily forgotten with Drake's comment. He chuckled. "What you can't say no to is her tongue. At least, that's what I hear every time you spend the night with her and show up for work with a cocky-ass grin that won't quit."

Drake nodded toward the cruiser's cabin at Nick's back. "'Bout time you had a cocky-ass grin of your own, I'd say."

He *was* overdue for some excitement. It had been almost three weeks since he broke things off with Anna. She hadn't done it for him. Oh, she'd managed to slake his sexual appetite all right, but nowhere close to what he had a feeling the blond honey downstairs could do.

Outside of the bedroom, Anna hadn't done much for him either. He needed a woman he could laugh with when the acrobatics were over. The only time he'd laughed over anything where Anna was concerned was the time she'd said his sister had her life in perfect order for someone so young. Emily and order in the same sentence, now that was a goddamn riot.

"In case you've forgotten, sleeping with the guests is a good way to get kicked outta the resort permanently," Nick reminded himself as much as the other man.

It was Drake's turn to laugh. "Do you think anyone actually follows that rule?"

Yeah, for some reason he had. "You don't?"

He shrugged. "Sure, I do. More often than not," he added with a smirk. "Why do you care about the rules anyway? I thought you were going to take that news offer."

"I might." He'd be considering the full-page world news spread a hell of a lot harder if not for his sister. The job included travel, and that meant leaving Emily home to her own devices. If leaving a horny as hell nineteen-year old home alone for weeks on end wasn't scary, then nothing was. At the same time, she was an adult, and he had his own life to lead.

At thirty-three, he wasn't getting any younger. Time and again, he'd passed over better paying and more respectable job opportunities to stay in the area and see to his sister's welfare. And then there were those far more enticing opportunities, he thought, with a backward glance at the lower level stairwell

"The way I see it, that little hottie couldn't have come along at a better time," Drake said. "You already plan to quit this job. With no worry over getting canned, you can spend the whole weekend thinking of ways to get at her can."

Nick let loose a pained laugh. He didn't need the whole weekend to contemplate ways to get at Stephie's ass. He'd figured out a dozen or so watching her walk away. The erection he'd only just managed to calm, emerged with renewed vigor at the recollection of her firm backside as she scooted down the dock.

He had to admit there were worse ways to spend the weekend than with his limbs twined around a gorgeous blonde. If he knew for sure he'd be taking that news position, the answer wouldn't be that difficult at all.

Nice guy or not, the longer he sat here, remembering the way her breasts plunged over the top of her shirt, beckoning to fill his hands, and the harder his cock got, the more certain he was he wanted every bit of what she offered.

What if he went for it, spent the weekend enjoying both Stephie's and the cruiser's amenities, and then the news job ended up falling through? Not a problem unless someone high enough up in the resort chain found out and took action. He might not need this job for the money, but he sure as hell valued the time it allowed him to spend on the water.

"Fuck, I don't know," he ground out. "She's tempting, I'll give you that."

Drake's eyes widened and he nodded. "Yeah, I'd say she is."

Nick glanced back in the direction of the other's man stare, and it took every bit of his self-control to keep his tongue in his mouth. Stephie wasn't naked, but she might as well have been. Her breasts pressed firmly against the tiny bikini top that covered them. No, that wasn't true. The tiny patches of black leather held together by strings at her back and neck covered her nipples and that's about it.

The strap of leather at her crotch wasn't much better. If she wasn't shaved, then she had a damn neat trim job going on. Though she stood facing him, he guessed the bikini bottom was of the thong variety. Damn if the thought of pulling that strip of leather tight against the crack of her ass didn't make him ready to beg to do just that.

Drake stood and slapped him on the back. "I need to get going. Alexis is waiting, and I hate to keep her simmering for long." He quirked a knowing eyebrow. "Good luck this weekend. Don't do anything I wouldn't do."

Knowing Drake's appetite, that didn't leave out much.

Still, Nick would take the luck. He'd need every bit of help he could get if he had any hope of staying the wills and wants of his way too desirable companion. "Thanks, Matson. See you Sunday night." *I hope.*

The way that Stephie was looking at him, like she was ready for dinner and he was the main course, by Sunday there probably wouldn't be much more left to him than a pair of canvas shorts and the remains of his quickly deteriorating brain cells.

"Ready to shove off?" Nick asked her as he stood, his voice rich with the lust that stirred through his body and caged his racing heart.

"Am I ever." She stepped toward him, stopping a couple feet away and licked her lower lip. "Just tell me what I can to do help, captain. For the next forty-eight hours, your every wish is my command."

That's exactly what he was afraid of, Nick thought as he inhaled her spicy hot cinnamon scent. All it would take was one word of encouragement and she'd be all over him like a dog in heat. Hmm…doggie style. Cramming his erection between her tight butt cheeks and clutching her hair in his fists while he rode her for all she was worth, was liable to be one of the most memorable experiences of his life. It was also bound to be the end of his weekends aboard the *Hidden Desire*.

Until he decided one way or another on the world news offer, he'd best keep his brain as far from his cock as possible. That wasn't going to be easy, considering his cock was hightailing it ever farther north. Pretty soon his shirt would be pushing over his waistband. Once that happened there'd be no way he could deny how badly he wanted to taste her offered-up flesh and suck at her skin until every trace of cinnamon was replaced by the heady smell of sex.

* * * * *

The telltale tilt of her Adonis's erection was a sure sign that he still wanted her. His voiced 'she's tempting' was all the further encouragement that Stephie needed. For just a second as she stepped up onto the deck and felt the dry summer heat settle into her lungs, she'd been nervous. Then she'd heard his words, and her tension was replaced with excitement over the long weekend to come.

And they would come. Both of them. Numerous times.

With a confident smile, she tossed the mooring lines to the stranger's friend, who waited on the dock, and the cruiser started away from the harbor. She stood at the back of the boat with her arms wrapped around her in an eager hug as the shore slowly disappeared. Good bye naked resort people, hello naked boat people.

Reaching the end of the no-wake zone, the cruiser spurred into action. Stephie took a seat on the back bench and stared up at the cockpit that dominated the boat's top level. Her weekend lover was up there, waiting for her to come visit him.

She tucked her whipping hair beneath the thin bikini strap tied at her neck and laughed. More likely he was hiding out in fear she *would* come visit him. While his body had no trouble conveying what he wanted, and even his mouth for that one instant when he thought she wasn't listening, the rest of him sure didn't seem to want to give in. He'd kept a wide berth between them as he made his way up the stairwell a few minutes earlier.

He could keep his distance until they got out on the water. Once they stopped he owed her a tour and a detailed account of how to use all those interesting looking gadgets in the cabin below. She planned to make the most of his explanation and see if she couldn't get a few first-hand examples while she was at it.

* * * * *

Nick couldn't remember reaching the stretch of lake marked as *Hidden Desire's* so quickly in his life. He hadn't gone any faster than usual. If anything, he'd gone slower in the hopes of delaying Stephie's advances awhile longer.

They were out on the water now, where they would stay all weekend unless she opted to move to another spot or explore one of the nearby islands. And that meant his alone time was over—at least temporarily. He'd put off giving her the tour of the boat that usually happened before leaving shore. He'd needed time and distance from her, so he'd prolonged the inevitable. But now time was up, and he had a tour to give. If her actions so far were anything to go on, she wouldn't stop at a tour—she'd want a detailed explanation, if not an example, of how each and every sex toy worked.

Stephie was a bad girl doing her damnedest to bring out his inner bad boy. The bitch of it was she was doing a hell of a job. Already she had him wanting to break the rules, yearning to grab hold of her and not let go until he'd had his fill of her luscious body and spicy scent.

As if on cue, the bad girl in question emerged on the top step of the cockpit's stairwell. The majority of her long blond hair was tucked back behind her head, but a few strays framed her sun-kissed face. Her deep brown gaze on him, she slowly advanced. Nick watched the hypnotic sway of her hips as she edged ever closer, then stopped altogether a hair shy of touching his knees.

She leaned toward him, her big boobs straining beneath the material of her itty-bitty bikini top, her nipples puckered and oh-so-easy to make out through the fabric. His tongue moved in his mouth, longing to stroke over each full ripe bud in turn, then follow up with bites and sucks that made her twitch and lurch beneath him.

She bent further still, so that the edge of a dark pink areola escaped its confines and winked at him teasingly, temptingly. Erotically. His mouth went cotton dry and rational thought bounced away on the shallow waves that surrounded them.

His hand reached for her on its own accord. Realizing its intent an instant before he palmed her breast, he used his wandering fingers to tuck the stray hairs on the right side of her face behind her ear. Her ruby red lips lifted at the corners barely enough to acknowledge, but enough to make him realize how full and kissable they were.

Would she taste like a cinnamon-coated bad girl, or soft and sexy as sin?

Her lips lifted further into a dazzling smile that all but stole his breath and completely stole his common sense. His fingers drifted from her neck toward her breast, tingling in anticipation of grabbing hold of a succulent mound of naked flesh and not letting go unless she begged. Maybe he wouldn't even let go then. Maybe he'd take her into his mouth and feast on her until she dug her long nails into his back and screamed her ecstasy as she climaxed.

"So, you ready for that tour, captain?"

The sultry sound of Stephie's voice broke the mystical spell she'd been weaving since she stepped foot on his turf, and Nick just about fell out of his chair.

He jerked his hand back to his lap, straightened, and struggled for words. His gaze dropped from her chest in search of safer territory. He locked sites on the scrap of black leather that covered her femininity, and bit back a pained groan. Just thinking about the silky heat hidden beneath her bikini bottom had his cock pulsating with desire.

With effort, he stood and nodded his assent. Thank God, the English language made use of body language as well as words to convey a response. He didn't trust his mouth to say something he wouldn't live to regret, like how about we forget what I said earlier and do the nasty here and now?'

Stephie's mouth lifted into a wider grin than what he'd seen so far. Her eyes sparkling with rich humor, she looked down, in the direction of his groin. "You, ah, want some help with that?"

Nick followed her gaze to the erection that slammed up against his shorts and on an indrawn breath, realized exactly how well body language conveyed a response. He'd taken his shirt off during the cruise out to the lake and what he'd been trying to hide earlier now saluted them both.

Ah, Christ. "I think I can handle it," he bit out dryly.

"Let me know if you change your mind."

She'd be the first. "I won't."

She looked to his face, then back at his shaft. "Two days is an awfully long time."

Yeah, it was. And it seemed to be getting longer with each passing second. "It seems that way now," he said as calmly as he could manage, which wasn't very calmly at all, "but on Sunday you'll be wondering where the time went." He gestured toward the stairwell. "Let me show you around, so you can get busy doing…well, whatever it is you plan to do this weekend."

"I'm going to fuck myself."

The air squeezed from Nick's lungs and he gaped at her. Her cheeks were flushed with color, as if even she was astounded by the words, but her slightly amused, highly sexual grin belied any hint of embarrassment. *"Excuse me?"*

She lifted a lightly muscled shoulder. "Unless I find a willing partner, I think masturbation's about the only entertainment I have to look forward to this weekend."

"Right." She was going to fuck herself. Jesus, the woman had no shame at all. Damn if that wasn't the biggest turn on.

His cock pressed harder against his shorts in answer to the unspoken words. Stephie turned away and started down the stairwell, but not before he caught her glance at his hard-on and the knowing smile that curved her lips. She clearly thought it was only a matter of time before he gave in to her wicked ways.

His gaze narrowed on the strip of leather sheathed between her firm butt cheeks, and his body tightened with the thought of thrusting into that honeyed perfection. Drawing a long breath of lake air that did nothing to calm the raw need racing through him, he realized she was probably right—it was only a matter of time before he gave in. But that was up to him to decide. After all, it was his ass on the line.

Well, he amended with a feral smile, hers too if he had his way.

The image of her tight little body fogging his brain, Nick hobbled his way down the second and base deck stairwells to the cabin below. Stephie waited expectantly just inside the door.

He fought for nonchalance while he ached for anything but. "Did you have a chance to look around during the ride out?"

"No." She glanced around the large cabin, then back at him. "It's very black."

That was the understatement of the decade. "Most couples like it that way. There are light switches next to every door. Here." He pointed to a round circle that looked a lot like a glow-in-the-dark condom. Could be because that was the intention. "You flip these up and there's the switch." He flipped the switch. The room lit with a soft glow that crowned Stephie in an ethereal light unbefitting a naughty temptress like her.

"Clever." She closed the short distance between them and placed her hand over the finger he'd kept on the switch. A zillion and one jolts of awareness jetted up his arm and thickened his already too-hard cock.

"So—" her hot breath snaked along his ear "—if I stroke this little knob, the glow gets bigger."

"Yeah, that's the general idea," he choked out.

She moved her hand away, and Nick heaved a sigh of relief.

"Thanks for showing me...I don't think you ever told me what your name is."

That's because he feared waking up in the middle of night hearing her screaming it out as she came. It was bad enough that he figured his own nights would be filled with wet dreams of her and her saucy mouth and scrumptious body.

He hesitated before conceding, "Nick."

"Nick." The corners of her lips turned up. "Rhymes with dick. That ought to be easy to remember. So, Nick, what else do you have to show me?"

A whole hell of a lot if she kept up with the dirty talk. "Let's start in the bedroom."

"If that's where you like to do it...the tour, I mean."

"That's where I normally start."

Nick marched past the large galley into the bedroom, his job concerns lessening with every step. He gazed at the king-sized bed glorified in black silk with white and black pillows. It would be so damned easy to toss her back on that bed and fuck her until she forgot her own name, let alone goading him with sexual quips.

He yanked open the drawer beside the bed instead, and did a quick inventory of the supplies the resort stocked for this weekend's getaway. Soft, full breasts rubbed against his naked back and cinnamon exploded in his senses. He checked the urge to swivel back on her, knowing if he did they'd be torso to breasts, pelvis to stomach. In other words, too damned close for his brain to function on all cylinders.

Stephie's arm shot beneath his, stroking his side and upper arm with wispy fine hair, and grabbed a small white canister from the drawer. She held it up in front of him, and read the label next to his ear. "Coochie cream?"

"In case you need to do a, ah, touch-up shave." Shit, he sounded like an idiot. This part of the cruise was second nature to him. At least it was when it was a bubbling honey asking questions about items she planned to use with or on her mate.

Stephie might be a honey, but she didn't have a mate. For now anyway.

She brushed her breasts against his side, her erect nipples prodding into his flesh, and sank down on the bed, straddling his half-turned body. Nick stared at her parted legs and held his breath, waiting for her next move, wishing to hell he wasn't so excited to find out if it involved him.

With a wink, she grasped her right calf and lifted her leg onto the silk coverlet. Angling it, so her splayed thighs were wide open for his viewing pleasure, she ran her fingertips up its length. She reached her knee and started the slow journey down, way down until the tips of her nails reached the hollow at her bikini bottom. Her lips lifted as she stroked her fingers back and forth along the suit's edge.

"I don't think I'll need a touch up shave," she said huskily, her cheeks flushed with what he guessed to be the same excitement flaming inside him, clamoring for release. "At least not here." Her fingers continued lower still and he gasped aloud when they sank beneath the leather covering her crotch and disappeared out of sight.

The leather twitched as her knuckles beaded against the suit's inside, the remainder of her fingers buried deeply in a place that took a better man than him not to imagine, or for that matter wish they were his own. Hell, he could picture her quivering pussy so damned easily — layers of soft pink shimmering with her juices and in the center of all that heat, a puffed up clitoris just waiting for his caress.

Her ministrations increased and she let free a rolling moan of pleasure as her shoulders tensed and shuddered. Her eyes bright, she pulled her fingers free of the bikini bottom with a slurping sound that foretold her wetness. The smell of her sex reached his nose, and he breathed it in like a dying man.

"Nope, not here either," she said a little breathless. Her grin came slowly, almost shakily, and she reached an opened hand toward him. "So...do you want to check too, just to be sure?"

Holy fuck. I'm in deep shit.

Nick resisted the urge to scrub his hands over his face, and looked back at the drawer without seeing a thing but the vision of her wet, hot core. She'd already gotten herself ready, all he had to do was grab hold of her hips and slide his cock in until she couldn't take him any further. If her pussy lips were as tight as her ass, he'd be lucky to make it all the way in before he came. Shit, if she kept up with the masturbating he'd be lucky to make it out of the room before he came.

His heart hammering and his erection so hard he feared it might go off with the simplest touch, he stared past the blind haze that consumed him and locked sights on the lover's dice. His hand trembled as he reached for the red and white dice engraved with words instead of dots. He scooped them up and rolled them onto the bed in front of her. The words that popped up had him clenching his hands into fists.

Stephie drew her other leg onto the bed and bent it at the knee. He could easily make out the darker shade of black at her crotch, the area he knew was saturated with her come, the same musky essence that clung to the air. He burned to fist that stretch of fabric in his hand and rip it from her body so he could drive into her slick wet folds, again and again until the need was forever gone from his mind.

She reclined back and ran a fingernail over each of the dice in turn. "Lick." Her tongue darted out, wetting the lower half of her pouty mouth, then jetted back between her luscious lips. She quirked an eyebrow as she moved her finger to the other dice and read its words aloud, "Below the waist."

Without so much as a pause, her hand journeyed back down to that dangerous zone from where it had only just emerged. This time she didn't bother sliding her fingers beneath the leather, she stroked herself right in front of his eyes.

Increasing the pace of her fingers to a frantic level, her chest rose and fell rapidly and her breathing grew sporadic and untamed. Nick's own breathing registered too loud in his ears, then stilled completely when with a cry of rapture, her fingers went limp and her head lolled back. The dark area on her suit grew darker yet and he released a loud, long groan of incredulity and appreciation.

Two days was a hell of a long time, and he was in deeper shit than he'd even guessed.

Stephie rose to a sitting position and slid her legs over the side of the bed. She edged toward him, until her damp thighs pressed intimately around the muscles of his leg. When she spoke her voice was thick with every bit of the pleasure she'd just given herself. "I don't think I can lick below my own waist." She picked up the dice and held them out to him. "So, I guess I'll have to put these back for someone with a partner."

Nick didn't miss the silent question. *Did he want to be it?* He also didn't miss the way his cock bobbed in a responsive *'Yes, please, please may I be it?'*

Stephie didn't miss it either. She flashed those dazzlingly white teeth of hers and reached for his erection. "I think someone wants to play."

Chapter 3

Stephanie nearly sighed aloud when Nick pulled back before she could make contact with his undulating penis. Stephie refused to allow that relieved sound to leave her lips. But even bad girl Stephie had to concede what she'd done in front of him went way beyond the bad she'd had in mind. At least, for this stage in the game.

The kind of show she'd put on was supposed to be reserved for day two and then only when Nick was firmly tied down and unable to take part in her ministrations. But there was something about him — maybe the contrasts between the hungry horndog and the reserved rationalist — that made her too reckless, too daring for her own good. He made her do and say things she would never even think of around anyone else.

The way she'd boldly stated her plans for this weekend, for example. She couldn't believe the words had made it out of her mouth. She didn't talk that way, telling near strangers she planned to fuck herself. She sure as hell had never masturbated for an audience before. She thought she would have been too nervous to even enjoy it. Yet, for Nick, she could have gone on fondling herself for hours simply to watch the excitement deepen his sea green eyes, the tic of nerves at the corner of his strong jaw.

She'd definitely enjoyed herself. Watching him watch her was the biggest turn on she'd ever experienced. One she planned to repeat. Soon.

For now she needed to forget about the raw appetite that consumed her, tightening her nipples into hard, painful buds and building an endless supply of heat between her already too damp thighs.

No matter how badly she wanted Nick—and oh did she ever want him—she wasn't ready for him. She hadn't yet had time to get the wrist and ankle cuffs in place. While the new Stephie might be audacious with words and maybe even actions, she wasn't daring enough to take him without restraints. She had to stay in control, be the one calling the shots. She had to remember she was the dominator here, and not give him the opportunity to think any differently.

Nick slammed the toy drawer closed and veiled the want that had burned brightly in his eyes. Too bad for him he couldn't veil the want the rest of his body exhibited— too bad for her too. It would be so much easier to forget about his hard-on if it wasn't sticking out at her, begging for her touch, or maybe her kiss.

"Something tells me you can check out the rest of this stuff all by yourself," he said gruffly and started out of the bedroom.

"Does that mean the tour's over?" Stephie asked innocently, following him.

"Food's served three times a day," he ground out in way of an answer. "Nine a.m., then noon and six with the exception of tonight. Friday dinner is served at eight unless you've already eaten and wanna skip it altogether."

Food? She hadn't even thought of that staple since leaving Greg's apartment complex earlier today. Her stomach rumbled now in angry protest of her oversight.

"I'm starving," she admitted, her mouth all but watering as she recalled the tantalizing dishes detailed in the *Hidden Desire's* brochure. She'd expected the boat to be staffed with a chef. She'd been wrong. And that meant Nick did all the cooking.

Impressive. Not only was the man built like an Adonis, he had culinary skills.

He came to a stop in the center of the galley, and Stephie stared at the hard, defined ridges that lined his naked back. Her fingers itched with the need to trace over the sinewy muscle. She stepped closer to him, but resisted the urge to touch.

The way he'd pulled away from her in the bedroom when she'd been so sure he'd been raring to go, had her second-guessing her strategy. Maybe he was the type of guy who needed a little getting-to-know-each-other time before the festivities began.

The old Stephanie could certainly relate to that. The new Stephie was more than willing to share in conversation, and she might as well start with the subject of his 'magical disappearance'. "You said back on the shore that once we make it out here, I won't see you again the rest of the weekend. How will I get my food?"

Nick turned back and shot her a surprised look, like he couldn't believe she'd been listening when he'd explained how the weekend getaway worked. "There's a delivery system similar to a dumbwaiter behind the panel next to the refrigerator." He gestured toward a small rectangular door that looked like it would house a cupboard. "Behind that door's a hollow shaft." He tripped over the last word, then added, "Your food will show up there. When you finish eating, put your dishes back inside."

She went to the panel he'd indicated, leaned against the counter beneath it, and pulled open the door. She stuck her head into the small space and stared up. Light filtered at the top, but beyond that she couldn't make out a thing.

"Does this lead to your cabin?" she asked, glancing back at him.

His gazed narrowed. "Yeah, but it's not big enough to fit a person."

Stephie almost laughed out loud. She'd honestly been curious how the whole system worked, she hadn't planned to pull herself up into his room and attack him in his sleep. But now that he'd mentioned it...

Her gaze dropped to his firm abdominal muscles. A dark line of hair snaked its way down from his navel and disappeared into low-slung shorts. His erection no longer sprouted out, but she could still imagine it, standing tall and thick and strong, waiting for her attention. It made her mouth water all over again. It also made Nick groan. Maybe the animalistic sound had more to do with the fact she was staring at his penis like it was her favorite new plaything, or possibly her dinner.

The old Stephanie nearly blushed at the realization, but the new Stephie wouldn't let her. The new Stephie slid her gaze back to Nick's and purred, "Thanks for saving me the trouble of finding out myself. I'd hate to be stuck in there all weekend when I could be—" She grinned slowly, slyly, then shifted her gaze toward her crotch " —enjoying myself."

Without so much as batting an eye, he said curtly, "Remember, you're welcome to use anything you find in this cabin, but once you play with it, it's yours. That means the price of it gets tacked on your bill."

Her grin faltered at his lack of response. She thought she'd at least get a nervous twitch out of him. Apparently, she really was going to have to reel him in with pre-pillow talk. It was just as well. She needed to know a few things about him before they locked limbs and swapped bodily fluids. Certainly not his life story, but a few details, like if he had a girlfriend or, worse, a wife. She might be hungry for all Nick had to offer, but she'd never stoop to sleeping with someone else's man.

"The drinks you ordered when you reserved your weekend are in the refrigerator," he continued his spiel, his tone monotonous. "If you run outta anything, jot down what you need and send it up with the dirty dishes." He hesitated, then crossed his arms over his broad chest and eyed her meaningfully. "There should be absolutely *no* reason for in-person contact until we dock Sunday night."

Was that supposed to be a warning? Stay away or else? Or else what?

Frankly all the ways that Stephie could think of for him to get even for disobeying him excited her more than anything else. As far as no in-person contact, that wouldn't be possible, since they'd be sharing dinner in his cabin tonight.

Determined to set his too strict mood askew, she sank against the counter and leaned on her crossed arms in a way she knew all but pushed her boobs out of their pint-sized holders. Unlike her earlier move, this action had the desired effect. His gaze wavered to her breasts then snapped back to her face and he scowled.

"Wow, Nick," she drawled. "You really have all the bugs worked out, huh?"

"I've been doing this for a long time."

And not one woman in all that time had propositioned him? With his rippling pecs, tall firm body, and killer smile, that was hard to believe. Or maybe women had come on to him and he'd ignored their offers. If he had, he must have been more convincing with them than he was with her. She didn't believe for a second he wasn't thinking about the way she'd stroked herself back on that bed. Just like she didn't believe he wasn't dying for another glance at her chest.

He turned on his heel. "I have things to do. Enjoy your weekend."

"So, I guess this is goodbye?" She didn't have to fake the sorrow in her tone. She really would miss him. He did more than rev her engine. He amused, excited and intrigued her all at once. If she'd come on this boat to meet a man, and not just to get lucky, she might actually consider taking the chemistry between them seriously.

But she had come here to get lucky, and a serious relationship was the last thing she wanted. Today, or anytime in the foreseeable future.

Nick glanced back at her, his brow knit as if he'd caught the regret in her tone and was confused by it. "It's the end of the tour if that's what you mean."

"Two days is an awfully long time," she repeated her earlier observation, pressing her arms even tighter together. She wanted him to burn for her body, not question her motive for being here in the first place.

"So you said."

She licked her bottom lip and lowered her lashes. "If I get lonely —"

"There's a phone on the nightstand next to the bed," he bit out. "Call Greg."

Stephie flinched. Unwanted hurt pressed at her heart and good girl Stephanie threatened to break free complete with sorrowful tears. Without warning, a sniff escaped her, and mystification stole over Nick's face.

With an inward curse, she curbed her tumbling emotions and straightened. She would not allow this weekend to be ruined by her meddling better half.

He took a step toward her, and his perplexity turned to outright compassion. He looked like he wanted to offer her a shoulder to cry on, Stephie realized with a stab of admiration that quickly faded to regret. There was no time for Nick to care about what happened between her and Greg, or her and anyone for that matter. The weekend was already blazing past and so far all they'd shared was a handful of words and a joint desire to get down and dirty. A desire only one of them was owning up to.

She tossed back her shoulders and forced a carefree grin into place. "Greg and I are over. I got tired of him."

Nick stared at her another moment then dragged his hand through his hair, sending the thick, black waves into chaos. "Then call someone else, just don't call..." He gave his head a firm shake. "Never mind. Your dinner will be down in an hour."

Her grin became sincere at the thought of dinner. It was just plain stupid to wallow over the loss of a man like Greg when she had a man like Nick to share her meals and oh so much more with.

She approached him slowly, but with a purposeful stride, stopping bare inches from his rigid form. Tipping her head back, she met his turbulent eyes. "Thanks, Nick, and let me know if you need help with anything. Anything at all. Just say the words."

He took a step back into the doorway. "I don't—won't—I don't want your help."

She reached a hand to his bare forearm and trailed her long nails down the corded muscle. "In case you do though, I'm here for you."

He pulled his arm back. "Have a good weekend."

She pursed her lips and said with a confidence only Stephie could muster, "I'm spending it fucking myself, Nick, how could it not be good?"

Like a pendulum set free, his penis all but slammed into her belly.

She laughed. "Someone sure woke up quick."

He half-smothered a curse and hightailed up the stairwell. She eyed his taut ass appreciatively until he reached the main deck and veered out of sight. The sense of impending victory pumped through her blood and further moistened her bikini bottom.

Nick would come around soon, she knew. No man could resist the lure of carnal temptation forever. In case he was stronger than most, she'd be sure to bring a little added incentive to dinner tonight.

* * * * *

Nick uncovered the shallot, bay leaf and oil mixture and added in the veal cutlets, his mind in a jumble. Given the choice between his mind being in a jumble and buried somewhere between his cock and balls, he'd take the jumble.

Stephie had him more than a little confused. For just a minute back in her room, he'd seen a glimpse of the nice girl he'd first guessed her to be. She'd looked completely dejected at the mention of Greg. He'd felt so bad for her at that moment he'd nearly pulled her into his arms. And wouldn't she have loved that?

Hell, maybe she would have appreciated a shoulder to cry on. She hadn't looked ready to maul him right then. She'd looked heartbroken. Was that sensitive woman the real Stephie, or was it the hellcat without a single ounce of shame? It pissed him off to no end that he wanted to know the answer so damned bad.

She was a stranger, a bad girl, or maybe a good girl in bad girl's clothing. She meant nothing to him. She was merely a guest aboard the *Hidden Desire*, nothing more or less. Now if he could disconnect his penis from his brain he might remember that.

A sharp rap sounded on the cabin door, scattering his thoughts.

Sonofabitch. He knew he hadn't seen the last of her, but he'd hoped she'd stay away for at least a couple hours, long enough for him to remember why this job mattered.

He turned up the heat on the skillet then stalked to the door. *"What?"*

"I thought maybe you could use some help with dinner."

Yeah right, she wanted to help with dinner. More like make him the main course. Besides, he'd already refused her offer of help. Of course, when it came to Stephie, 'no' didn't seem to be in her vocabulary. "No. I don't need any help."

"Are you sure? Because I'm a really good cook."

Yep, it wasn't in her vocabulary. Persistence sure as hell was though, Nick realized an instant later when he pulled open his door to see Stephie sucking on a beer bottle. Scratch that, a short, fat plastic cock bottle topper.

He should have known she'd find the topper drawer. The pecker popper and nipple sipper were guest favorites.

She let free her lip lock on the phallus, and shoved a second beer toward him that sported the nipple sipper. "I figured you could use some cooling off."

"Thanks," he ground out for lack of a better response and took the offered drink.

She replaced her mouth on the topper and hummed as she glanced past him. Any illusion he had she might be a good girl in bad girl's clothing died away.

Her lips made a slurping sound as they released the tip of the sipper, and he was transported to that moment back on her bed when she'd removed her fingers from her pussy. She'd been so wet, so ready for him. How the hell he'd ever resisted the urge to toss her back and fill her until she screamed his name was beyond him. He didn't want to resist her now. He wanted to replace that plastic penis in her mouth with his own.

She ran her tongue over the rim of the sipper and he grunted in the back of his throat. Damn, he wanted her. Wanted her in a way that belied every claim he'd ever made about being a nice guy.

Nice guys didn't have the kind of thoughts he was having now, nice guys didn't want to ram their cocks straight up her tight little ass and grip her butt cheeks so hard they'd bear his fingerprints for weeks. They sure as hell didn't want to come in her saucy red mouth until it overflowed.

"So, can I come in?" she asked.

Could she ever and while she was at it she could stay for dinner...and dessert.

Her face lit up and she flashed a smile that showed her perfect teeth. She ran her nails down his arm. "Why, Nick, that's so sweet of you to offer. I'd love to."

He gaped at her hand, wondering if anyone had ever taught her the rules of personal space. Her words sank in then. "What?"

"You asked me to stay for dinner..." Her brown eyes sparkled. "And dessert."

Ah, Christ. Had he really said that out loud? Score one for the peter, zero for the brain. Speaking of which, thank God he'd had the good sense to put on a shirt before making dinner, because his erection was back in all its glory.

Stephie brushed past him, and he inhaled the scent of jasmine. He'd resisted the urge to lick the cinnamon from her supple body; he didn't feel like resisting this scent as well. He felt like giving in. It would be so simple. A single yes and she'd have her long legs wrapped around his neck and her sweet, hot sex dripping honey on his face.

"Nice place," she said, making what sounded remarkably like conversation.

Nick stared at her firm backside with nothing more than the strip of leather covering it, and sighed. He was hard as a rock and all but ready to give into her wildest fantasies, and now she wanted small talk. If that wasn't just like a woman.

Still, it was kind of nice to hear she liked his place. It was also a rude awakening to why he needed to resist her. The mostly glass and window-enclosed cabin was his second home. Sometimes more like his first. He savored the time he spent tucked away in his own little glass world with the lake breeze rolling in and no immature sister to bail out of her most recent catastrophe.

One misstep with blondie and he could lose it all. Of course, he might lose it all anyway. If he took that news offer, he wouldn't get out on the lake for some time. At the same time, if he took that news offer and the sizable raise that accompanied it, he'd be able to afford his own pleasure cruiser. And he could have blondie, any which way he wanted until Sunday night rolled around.

He shrugged and started for the stove. "The cabin's all right."

She flashed him what looked to be an honest to goodness smile. This one didn't make her look like a piranha desperately in need of a hunk of meat, but an amused, approachable woman. "I'd trade it for my dungeon any day."

"You have lights," he pointed out, not wanting to like the way she looked when she wasn't trying so hard, or the fact that at this moment she seemed not only nice, but slightly intelligent.

Stephie slid into the seat of the wall side booth and set her beer bottle on the table. "Condom-covered. I remember."

Nick frowned at her as he stirred the veal and sauce mix. This conversation just kept getting more and more normal. Yeah, they were discussing condoms, but she hadn't even made a single crack about ways they could use them. What the hell was she up to? And did he really want to know?

He grabbed his beer from where he'd set it on the counter near the small stove and sat in the booth across from her. He could manage small talk as much as the next guy, the secret was to keep his eyes above her neck. One glance at her full-to-bursting breasts and his good intentions were liable to go out the window.

"So, what do you do for a living, Stephie?" he asked, tipping his beer to his lips.

"I'm a financial analyst for Gamble & Net."

He almost dropped his drink. No way, this young woman, scratch that, sex pistol had a brain to go with her killer body? Two seconds ago he thought he'd detected some intelligence, but still... Could he have been wrong about the whole daddy's girl thing? Had she bought that Beemer out of her own pocket? Nah, couldn't be.

"You're fucking with me," he said.

With a wink, the vixen he was quickly coming to know returned. She took a long thorough pull from the plastic penis, then sank down in her seat and rubbed her bare foot up his leg. Her powerful toes kneaded his tensed muscles, the short nails nipping hungrily into his bared flesh as they edged ever higher in search of his shaft.

"Trust me, Nick," she breathed huskily, "you'll know when I'm fucking you."

He bit back a groan as her foot skimmed past the edge of his shorts and fondled his balls with a rough caress. Stroking the length of his hard, pulsating cock, she quirked an eyebrow. The raw need in her tone when she spoke next sped his already racing heart. "You really shouldn't avoid the inevitable, Nick."

Knowing too damned well how right she was, how slim the odds were he'd survive this weekend with his mentality intact unless he gave in to her hedonistic advances, he sank lower in his seat, closed his eyes and moaned his appreciation. Fuck the job. Even if he lost both the news offer and his captain's position the worst that would happen was he'd be stuck spending weekends home with Emily.

Whatever the outcome one thing was clear—it was time for Nick to find some excitement in his dull existence. Lately, he'd become bored with even his weekend life, and he realized now that Stephie was the reason. He'd been waiting for her to come along and shake up his world. She was here, and he was more than ready to take on any physical challenge she tossed his way.

Chapter 4

"You're used to getting your way, aren't you, Stephie?" Nick asked, opening his eyes to reveal a determined glint. Determined to get rid of her attentions, or determined to give in to them, Stephie couldn't tell.

He removed her foot from between his thighs and a tidal wave of disappointment washed through her. Determined to get rid of her attentions, she realized with a quiet pout. Damn, she really thought she had him that time. He'd even closed his eyes and moaned. Maybe he'd only been taunting her with the sensual sound, but it sure hadn't seemed like it. His large, straining cock beneath her sole definitely hadn't felt like it.

He stood and started for the stove. She scooted back up in her seat and stared after him. Had she lost him completely? Moving her foot away was one thing, but now was he dismissing her altogether?

"I'm not used to hearing no if that's what you mean," she said with a sexy bravado. She wasn't used to hearing yes either, but he didn't need to know that.

Stephie caught his amused laugh; it sounded mellow, yet aroused. Maybe he hadn't been trying to get rid of her after all, just playing another hand in this game she'd begun. If that was the case, then who was she not to follow his lead?

Joining Nick at the stove, she lifted her nails to his back and stroked him through his T-shirt. He jerked at her touch, but the flinch was well worth it. His heated skin and impressive muscles felt incredible beneath her fingertips. They would feel even more amazing when there was nothing but air separating her hands from the hard contours of his body.

"So, what about you?" she breathed near his ear.

He glanced back at her before lifting the skillet lid and turning over the meat that sizzled inside. "What about me?"

"Are you used to getting your way?"

He set the lid back, swiveled and leaned against the stove. He crossed his arms over his broad chest and the right side of his mouth tipped up in a cocky grin. Mirth rallied through his eyes. "I'm not used to hearing no if that's what you mean."

His words had been coated with a sexual confidence that skittered over Stephie's nerves as a silent warning. Stephanie emerged with a frantic leap that forced her to take a step back. What in God's name had just happened? Had Mr. Close Enough done an about face? The slant of his mouth and his arrogant stance sure appeared that way.

"What, you don't have a comeback?" he asked.

No. Not a single one. *Shut up, Stephanie! Of course, we have a comeback.*

Pushing back her unease, Stephie squared her shoulders and stepped closer, so close her breasts almost brushed his chest. She flashed a smile that she hoped looked just as arrogant as his. "Oh, I have a comeback all right," she said in a low, suggestive tone, "but I figured you'd want to eat before you hear it."

He lifted an eyebrow, his expression growing more amused and equally confusing by the moment. "Really. And why's that?"

Good question. Why was that? Oh yeah…"Because it's a visual."

"A visual?" This time he looked confused.

She had to hold back a victory shout. About time they had the tables turned back to how they should be. "Yeah, a visual," she purred, placing her palms flat on the solid planes of his chest. "It involves more than words…it involves touch. In lots of…shall we say…naughty places."

His confusion vanished as hunger stole through his sea green gaze. She didn't have to look down to know his penis was growing thicker and longer with each of their words, the tip of it grazed her naked thigh and made her bikini bottom so wet she felt as though she'd taken a swim on the way up to his room.

"Naughty, huh?" he questioned, his tone heavy with lust. "And what if I say no, that I don't want you to touch me in those…naughty places?"

"I didn't say anything about touching *you* in those…naughty places. But now that you mention it…" She licked her lower lip and ran her palms up his chest and around his shoulders until her breasts had no choice but to rub against his hard body. Not that she minded the way they grew more sensitized with each subtle brush of body against body. In fact, she enjoyed it very much. Nearly as much as she enjoyed the feel of his shaft sliding along the damp, scantily covered folds between her thighs.

Her pulse racing with the intimate sensations, Stephie tipped her head back and eyed his mouth. "We could touch each other." *Or kiss.* He had to be an amazing kisser. His lips were sculpted perfectly for the act.

Nick lifted her arms away from his body and set his hands on her shoulders. He moved his rough palms down her sides, until the edges of his big fingers grazed along the outsides of her breasts and had her nipples and most the rest of her body, swollen and burning for his touch.

"Dessert," he uttered.

"What?" she breathed, her brain hazing over as his thumbs drifted in slow circles toward the center of her breasts. He stopped centimeters from her distended nipples and she bit her lip to stop from moaning. She couldn't move, couldn't breathe. If his hands didn't finish their journey she was bound to implode just the way she accused Greg of doing if he didn't get sex.

Dear God, had Greg been right? Was it possible to implode without sex? It sure as hell felt like it.

Nick bent his head so close she knew he was going to kiss her. She licked her lips in anticipation, secret thrills coiling in her belly. The dangerous desire to forget about restraints and take him on the cabin floor chased through her.

He stilled then, his fingers and mouth so close and yet not nearly close enough. She wanted him touching her, stroking her, biting her. She wanted to feel his hard cock inside her, penetrating deep and hard, again and again, until she came with a scream.

He remained motionless, simply taking her in. In that moment, Stephie knew without a doubt a person could burst from sexual tension alone. "Nick…" she pleaded. *Do something. Touch me. Kiss me.*

Screw that, I'll do something.

She started to reach for him, to finally sate the desperate need to taste him, to attack his mouth with her tongue. Before she could make contact, he lifted his hands from her body, took a step back, and flashed a knowing grin. "Dessert, Stephie. After dinner we can touch each other. For now, hands off."

Stephie nearly whimpered at the loss of contact, then his words reached her and she gaped at him, her smile huge. Oh my God, he'd given in! He was going to be her sex slave for two whole days! She was going to get laid, to finally scratch her seven-year itch. And it was going to be with Nick.

Her smile faltered with her next thought. How would she get him down to her cabin and tied up to her bed? She had to get him there somehow, because no matter how much the idea of taking him on his cabin floor sounded like fun, she knew better than to allow it to actually happen.

There was no way Stephie could handle a man like Nick without restraints. He was too big, too virile, and though he'd attempted to keep her at bay originally, she knew now that he'd admitted he wanted her too, he'd expect to be the one in control. His teasing actions said as much.

Maybe, she'd get lucky and he'd go down easy once he heard the kind of fantasies she had in mind. But maybe not.

"How about some wine?" she asked, moving back to the table and dropping into the booth she'd earlier occupied. "To set the mood," she quickly added.

More like to get him drunk. Or at least slightly buzzed. Surely, he'd be more willing to meet her carnal demands under the influence. As for her, she could certainly use something to ease the taut edge that claimed her head to toe.

"Sounds good. White would go best with dinner," he replied, his attention so completely on cooking she wondered if she actually did anything for him at all. His body seemed into her, but the way he shut her out so easily made her think his head didn't give a shit one way or the other.

That's the idea, dumbass. She smiled at bad girl's Stephie's much-needed reminder. Yeah, that was the idea. A man who wanted her physically with no strings attached. She was here to get laid, nothing more, nothing less. Perfect.

"Greg and I ordered…" She trailed off. She was not going to think about that two-timing sleaze-ball at a time like this. Greg had messed up royally and because of it, Nick was going to reap the rewards. Actually, both she and Nick were going to reap the rewards. Something told her Nick's bedside manner could outdo Greg's any day or night of the week. She would find out both day and night very soon.

Excitement replaced her unease, and she darted to her feet and for the door. "There's a bottle of Chardonnay in the refrigerator downstairs. I'll be right back."

* * * * *

Nick frowned as Stephie's retreating form glided past his open cabin windows, then disappeared out of sight. What the hell had just happened? He'd finally given himself the green light to give her all she wanted and more, and she'd all but done a tailspin in the other direction. Even before the mention of her ex whatever-he-was, she'd been acting out of sorts. Certainly not during that mind-boggling and testicle tightening foot massage, but right before and shortly after.

A goddamned financial analyst! Talk about mind-boggling.

There was so much more to the woman than what he'd have ever guessed. Damn, if he wasn't excited about learning each and every angle of her before this weekend was through. Especially those angles he'd had his hands on a moment before. Her breasts were lush and ripe and begging for him to squeeze and bite and suck them all night long. He would, gladly, right along with the rest of her tantalizing curves.

Thoughts of the night to come spinning through his head, Nick replaced the half-empty beer bottles with wineglasses and place settings. He'd just finished putting their dinner onto a serving tray at the small kitchen's counter when Stephie returned. If he thought she'd looked edgy when she left, she looked anything but now.

She stood inside the cabin's doorway, her eyes glowing with expectation and the bottle of wine gripped tightly in one hand. Her eat-'em-alive smile was back in full detail and told him she knew how good she looked in the nearly see-through red dress. She might even expect a compliment. If she did, who was he not to give her one?

"Wow. That dress is..." Scandalous. Mouthwatering. Going to get ripped off really soon. "Wow."

Stephie sauntered toward the booth, each of her moves revealing tanned shapely legs and the flare of her naked hips where the dress was slit on either side. Her breasts pushed at the top edge of the gown, her nipples more than a little apparent through the flimsy material, and his fingers itched to help them spill free of their confines and into his waiting palms.

"I'm not wearing underwear." A blush stole over her cheeks. She looked away and placed the wine bottle on the table as she sat. "I figured why bother when they'll be off in an hour anyway," she said, uncorking the bottle.

Yeah, why bother, Nick thought. This way he could think about her pussy beading with moisture all through dinner, staining the back of her slinky outfit and dampening the booth cushions the same way she'd dampened her bikini bottom below deck. Christ, he had to quit thinking about her finger fucking herself downstairs, or her cushion wouldn't be the only one getting wet.

She glanced back at him, her gaze hot and hungry. "Do you want to share a booth? If you're beside me, I can stroke you with my hand instead of my foot."

"Great." *Not great, moron. You'll be coming before dinner starts at this rate.*

She filled the wineglasses, then slid to the back of the booth and leaned against the wall. "Is there anything I can do to help?"

"Just relax and get ready."

Her lips twitched. "Oh, I'm ready."

Yeah, so was he. Ready to come in his shorts.

Nick looked down at his faded canvas shorts and realized how underdressed he was for this momentous occasion. After all, it wasn't every day he broke company rules and his own personal mantra regarding sex with strangers. For all that he was laying on the line she'd better be damned good in the sack.

He lifted his head to find Stephie staring at him, her expression amused. "If your clothes make you uncomfortable, take them off."

Good thinking. Yeah right. "I'm comfortable."

"Then put dinner on the table and sit down." She patted the seat beside her, and her red-hot lips curved. "My hand's bored."

Right. Put dinner on the table. Her hand was bored. And he was horny as a teen on prom night. If he followed her lead, this night would progress along fine. If he followed his own lead, then the fun would be over before dinner was even served. He wanted to grab hold of her and grind his shaft into her lithe body right this second. That couldn't happen. Not yet anyway. A little hand fun though, now that might be right up his alley.

He sidled over and dropped down in the booth beside her, flashed a grin as he reached for her slender fingers. "What does your hand want to do, Stephie?"

Apprehension flashed through her eyes. Her smile fell away as she glanced past him to the stove. "You forgot the food."

"What does your hand want to do?" he repeated, pondering her reaction. Was she nervous, having second thoughts, scared of him? Shit, if she was any of the above, he never saw it coming. Or maybe he had. He thought she'd been edgy when she left the cabin, was she still?

Her throat bobbed, but her voice conveyed only raw desire. "I told you, Nick, it wants to stroke you."

"How?" he asked, searching for signs of the dirty-talking bad girl.

"Hard. And fast." She turned her hand in his and captured his first finger, ran her circled thumb and finger down the length of it, putting her words into action.

His cock responded to the simulation with a savage throb that had blood shooting like lightning toward his drawn balls.

Better, he thought of her teasing move, but still not quite good enough. Definite unease flared just past her confident words. If she wanted this, then she was going to have to say it, loud and clear. "Your hand wants to fuck me hard and fast?"

Her eyes flew wide. She quickly masked her surprise, but not quick enough. How authentic was her bad girl act? Was she bluffing with him? Had she been since the moment she stepped on his boat? And if so, why? Did she want to use him to get back at a guy she claimed to have grown tired of, or was there more to it than that?

"Do you want to fuck me, Stephie?" he pressed, needing to see how far she would carry out this charade, or if it were even a charade at all.

She nodded, lowered her lashes demurely, and said a soft, "Yes."

"Say it."

She licked her lower lip and raised her lashes, met his gaze. "I want to...I want to fuck you, Nick."

"With your hand while we eat dinner?"

The last shred of apprehension left her eyes, and she smiled. "Yes, Nick. I want to fuck you with my hand while we eat. And after we eat, I want to fuck you for real."

He smiled back at the brashness of her tone. She was either a damned good actress, or she was one hundred percent sincere. "Then I'd better sit on the left side. You're right-handed and I don't want you to starve while you're fucking me."

"Right." She flashed her teeth. "I need to build up my energy for dessert."

Nick's body hummed with anticipation as he retrieved the food from the counter. He slid into the booth past Stephie, inhaling her sultry scent as he went, then swiveled back to face her and lifted his wineglass. "A toast?"

She brushed her hair over her shoulder then raised her glass. "To new friends."

His lips quirked. "I was thinking more like, to one fucking great time. I can hardly wait to get my hands on your tight little ass."

A soft, strangled sound escaped her throat. She tossed back her wine, effectively drowning the noise, then saying in a throaty purr, "The feeling's mutual, captain."

Stephie set her wineglass down and forked a piece of veal into her mouth. She'd chewed for several seconds when a low moan drifted from her mouth. "Oh God, Nick! This is fabulous. What is it?"

"Fettine alla Melagrana," he answered, not bothering to keep the pride from his voice. Next to his waterside cabin, the biggest benefit of running the *Hidden Desire* was getting to use his culinary skills. That Stephie took the time to notice was a definite credit on her part. "My sister's favorite," he said absently.

She lifted her wineglass and eyed him wistfully. "I always wanted a sister. Is she younger or older than you?"

"Emily's younger." She was also the last person he'd meant to bring into this relationship, or whatever you wanted to call what he and Stephie had embarked upon.

She took a sip of wine then set the glass back. "How much younger?"

"More than a decade. She's nineteen."

Unidentifiable emotion passed through her eyes. "I hated that age," she said remotely, twisting her wineglass by its stem. "Too many choices to make, and they all seemed to lead in the wrong direction."

"When was it, last year?" Nick asked, genuinely interested in the direction their conversation had taken. Most particularly her age, and if she'd ever moved past that wrong direction phase. Or was that what he was? A choice she'd made that had led her in a direction she wasn't ready to follow through on. It would certainly explain her reversion to small talk.

"Seven years and twenty-three days to be exact," she said.

Twenty-six. Plenty old enough to make her own choices. As for her directions, it was time to figure them out. She'd acted like she'd wanted him since the moment she saw him, now he would learn how true those feelings were, or if the uncertainty he saw beyond her mask of sexuality would win out. "Well?"

She frowned. "Well what?"

He looked down at his lap to the hard-on that hadn't quit since they'd met. "Are you gonna talk all through dinner, or get to work?"

"Work?" she questioned tensely, her frown deepening.

So, she was still uncertain, was she? No way would he hold her to something she didn't want to do. He'd simply lay the cards on the table and let her decide how the game would play out. He lifted her left hand from where it rested on the seat near her thigh and settled it on his lap. "He wants to play, Stephie. You promised to fuck him during dinner and he's gonna get upset if you don't start pretty soon." He hesitated, before adding, "Or at least apologize for making him think you were gonna do something you aren't."

"Oh..." Her throat bobbed and she pulled her hand away.

Unexpected disappointment hit Nick square between the eyes. He shouldn't have been looking forward to spending the weekend indulging his every fantasy with his sexy companion, but he had been. He smiled past the regret, aware he'd called her bluff. He'd known the moment she stepped on that dock she was a nice girl. As he was always telling his sister, nice girls didn't sleep with complete strangers. Disappointed or not, they were both better off that she'd ended this game before things went any farther, and one or both of them ended up getting hurt.

Stephie took a long swallow of wine, mentally willing her courage into place. She could stroke him without restraints. So long as it was her hand on his body and nothing more, no one would be harmed. With a final sip, she set her glass back and moved her hand to his lap. On an indrawn breath, she smoothed the material of his shorts so that the outline of his extensive erection showed through. Wetting her lips, she twined her fingers around his thick shaft and met his eyes.

Nick gasped, his face riddled with disbelief. Triumph ran like heated liquid through her veins, strengthening her resolve as she took in his slackened jaw. He hadn't expected her to go through with it, she realized. Well, she had, and now that she had him within her grip, she wasn't making any promises about letting him go.

She flashed a wicked smile. "We don't want him to get upset, now do we, Nick?"

Savoring the control that charged through her, she ran her fingers the length of his burgeoning cock, once, twice. His shaft bobbed with the sensation, passion darkening his eyes to near midnight. And yet along with the passion was something that looked a whole lot like confusion.

"I never…" he started.

Expected her to be bold? Why wouldn't he think that, after the way she'd fondled herself in front of him?

"You never what?" she pressed when he remained silent.

"I've never wanted to come in someone's hand so bad in my life." All trace of confusion left his eyes and a cocky grin slanted his mouth. He lifted in his seat and slid his shorts down far enough to allow room for his penis to spring free. "Now touch me, sweetheart. Nothing in between, just skin on skin. Make me explode."

Stephie stared at his bulging shaft, any concern she had over his behavior fled as her mouth stripped of all moisture. She'd known he was built like an Adonis, she just never thought about his size extending to his manhood. While she'd seen only one other man in her life, it was safe to say Nick was bigger than most. He had to be eight inches or maybe even bigger than that. Maybe he wouldn't fit inside her body, but she couldn't wait to get her mouth on him.

As if he could read her thoughts, the deep purple head of his penis bobbed. She ran her tongue along the inside of her mouth, imagining the way he would taste, the way the ridges of his erect cock would feel sliding between her lips, his erection growing tense and slippery as come filled her throat. She'd wanted to have him that way since the moment she'd arrived at Murphy's Harbor, and now victory would soon be hers.

"Speechless, Stephie?"

No, dying with the need to take him between her lips and not let go until he climaxed. She could do that, because as was true with her hand, when her mouth was on him, she would be the one in control. No chance for anyone to get hurt. Perfect.

She looked to his face. "You're...equipped."

Nick raised a dark eyebrow, skepticism clear in his gaze. "Equipped? Are you trying to say I have a large cock?"

"Yeah. Yeah, you have a very large one."

"Say the words, Stephie. Don't be afraid."

"I'm not!" Just because she wasn't screaming out he had a big cock didn't mean she was afraid. She just didn't normally talk that way. Correction, Stephanie didn't talk that way. Stephie did. Somewhere between sitting down and him pulling out his penis, Stephanie had started to emerge. It was well past time she was put to rest.

"I'm not afraid," she assured, taking his hard sex into her hand. The warmth of his swollen member surged through her fingers and quickened her heartbeat. She needed this, needed to feel him within her grasp, the strength of him enfolded in her fist. His total and utter surrender as he found release at her hands.

He shot her a knowing look. "Then show me, sweetheart. You're paying for this weekend, put your mouth where your money is."

Sweeter words had never been spoken, Stephie thought, as she lifted the napkin from her lap and set it on the table. With a parting wink, she buried her head in his lap. She glided her lips gently over his throbbing shaft, savoring the tang of his salty flesh, the feel of power that radiated through his thin skin.

Lifting her head, she met Nick's eyes and smiled. She'd promised him a visual and she was more than ready to supply it. She laved a long, lusty swipe the length of his erection then purred, "It would be my pleasure to suck your cock, captain."

His eyes flashed wide and then lulled partially closed as she took the tip of him into her mouth. She drew her hand onto his lap and stroked the base of his sex where his pubic hair grew dense and dark and his balls drew tight. She took him deeper into her mouth and he groaned, fisting his hands in her hair.

Pulling back, she licked hungrily at the fluid that emerged on the head of his penis, the scent of sex, sweat and jasmine heavy in the air around them. "You taste incredible, Nick," she murmured. "You taste like more."

She took him between her lips again, then drove him into her mouth until she couldn't take any more. She hummed the way she had with that plastic bottle topper. Unlike the bottle topper, Nick didn't remain immobile. His grip on her hair tightened and his hips arched forward, thrusting him further into her mouth, beyond a limit she thought she could stand. She'd been wrong, she could handle as much as he wanted to give. She would take every inch of him if it were humanly possible.

"Ah, damn, sweetheart," Nick growled as his thighs grew taut beneath her.

Jerking spasms gripped his body, and he raked his fingers against her scalp. She knew he was about to climax and there was no way in hell she was going to budge until every last bit of his seed had spilled into her mouth.

His cock trembled between her lips and he released her hair, granting her free rein to move. She clung tighter, licking and sucking, stroking him harder and faster. Then in a blinding moment of pure ecstasy, he plunged hard into her mouth, his fingers tangling in her hair as he shouted her name. The fluid that raged through his body emptied into her mouth. She swallowed it quickly, milking every last drop from him with the force of her lips then finishing the job with a final, leisurely swipe of her tongue.

"Stephie…"

Hearing the apprehension in Nick's voice, she lifted her head and met his dark eyes, he looked pleased, but he also looked concerned.

He couldn't think she hadn't liked that? If he did he was seriously in need of an education. She licked her lips. "Mmm, captain, you seamen sure know your business."

A grin stole over his face, and she smiled back at him. "So, you ready for dinner?"

He shook his head, and his grin flowed over into his eyes. "Dinner can wait," he said, grabbing hold of her hand. "What I want is dessert."

Chapter 5

"What are you doing?" Stephie asked when Nick pulled her from the booth and started toward a door on the opposite side of the cruiser's cabin.

"You'll see," he said, his voice rough and his pace never faltering.

She gulped back her next words. She didn't want to see. It was her fault that he was dragging her through the cabin to parts unknown for...dessert.

Her heart beat faster at the thought of the forthcoming treat, of stripping his body bare and revealing every inch of his delectable flesh glistening from the combined heat of late afternoon and unbridled lust.

To unsheathe him one article of clothing at a time, sucking and licking each inch of muscled flesh as it was laid bare, would be beyond amazing. The only problem was he expected to do the same to her. And that couldn't happen.

That he thought it could was her doing. Her penance.

Good Lord Almighty, what the hell had she been thinking, dropping down in his lap and taking him into her mouth like that? She hadn't been thinking. At least not beyond how his erection would feel sliding into her mouth, his hot juices caressing the back of her throat. He made her too daring when he goaded her with his teasing words and tempting body.

Too daring—and stupid apparently.

She hadn't even taken the time to ask if he was married before she started sucking on him like there were no tomorrow. He couldn't be married. He wouldn't spend his weekends alone on a boat if he were, let alone be here with her now.

What about a girlfriend? With the size of his penis the man wouldn't have any trouble keeping a woman happy.

Nick released her hand and pushed open the door to reveal a bedroom. A large bed swaddled in pale blue was situated off to their right. Books, newspapers, a laptop computer and several photographs adorned the cubbyhole headboard.

Stephie's gaze locked on the photo of a young woman. It was hard to make out her eye color from this distance, but her facial features and coloring were too similar to Nick's to not make the connection it was his sister. She scanned the remaining pictures—a group of men with Nick in the middle, and another of an older couple.

She looked back at the first photograph, wondering if he was close with his sister. It would seem so since he kept her picture so near. What about the rest of his family? Did he get along with them? Or maybe he never saw them because they lived too far away, as was true with her parents.

So many questions she wanted to ask him, and yet she knew she shouldn't. Moreover, couldn't. Casual sex wasn't supposed to employ emotional and familial knowledge. Nothing beyond the existence of partners outside their group of two and how those partners would be affected by their coupling mattered here.

"Emily." Nick's husky words trailed along Stephie's neck and sent shudders rushing through her body, further tightening her already pebbled nipples. Shudders that made her too aware of what he thought was about to happen between them. What her own body begged her to let happen.

Between the dirty talk he'd coaxed out of her and feeling him come in her mouth, she was beyond wet. The swollen flesh of her vagina ached to allow him to enter and take all she had to give, until they were both breathless and covered in sweat.

Again she wondered if he would fit inside her. That hadn't been a worry with Greg. While they'd never made it to sex of any type, she'd felt his erection through his pants enough to know he was average if not on the slightly small side. The scene she walked in on in his bedroom confirmed her speculation on his size.

Nick wasn't like Greg in any way, shape, or form. Nick was equipped. Or as he liked to put it, had a very large cock. A very large, very sweet, very edible cock.

"Your sister's pretty," Stephie said, feeling the blush creep into her cheeks. Jeez, she couldn't even think naughty words without blushing. How she managed to speak them when Nick was facing her and not behind her as he was now, was beyond her. "She looks a lot like you," she added.

He chuckled, a rich rolling sound that further stoked the fire building inside her. The fire she longed to let him put out.

"Are you saying I'm a pretty boy?" he asked.

She swiveled at the incredulous statement. An arrogant grin tipped the corners of his sensuous mouth and dark stubble set off his strong jaw line. She took in the breadth of his shoulders and the finely honed muscles that stood out beneath his T-shirt, the hard, solid sinew she'd fondled with her foot before dinner, and her mouth went dry.

Nick was a lot of things. A lot of good, purely masculine, toe-tingling things, but pretty wasn't one of them. "No, of course not. I…"

"I was joking." He slid his lightly callused fingers back within her grip, and gave a tug followed by a sly wink. "Come on. Dessert's out here."

Stephie's pulse raced at the reminder she didn't need. "What about a wife?"

His grin faltered. "Now's a helluva time to ask."

"I…" didn't mean to — at least not quite that artlessly.

It was his bedroom that had her acting so base. Since the moment they stepped into it, Stephanie had been nipping at her heels, vying for a chance to speak. Most likely to say 'Get me the hell out of here while you still can'.

Squaring her shoulders, Stephie fought for bad girl spunk. She'd had it down pretty well for a while, how hard could it be to get it back? And once she had it back, how hard could it be to convince him they'd have more fun on her level of the boat?

She shook her hand free of Nick's and laid it flat on his chest. Tipping her head back to meet his eyes, she said in a throaty voice, "You don't have a wife. You wouldn't be here with me if you did." She paused and drew a courageous breath. "You wouldn't let me fuck you during dinner if you were married."

He smirked. The tic she'd noted when she'd masturbated in front of him, ignited in his jaw. She'd decided that he was irritated with her then, but now she wondered if the spasm were that of another kind. Of desire, and barely concealed appetite.

"Maybe I'm one of those guys who doesn't care."

Doom impounded the need within her, pushing back any headway she'd made on the naughty girl front. She squeaked out her next words. "Are you?"

He laid his hand over the one she'd placed on his chest, effectively swallowing hers beneath it. His gaze bore hungrily into hers. "I'm not married, or seeing anyone. I would've never let you go down on me if I was."

Thank God. At least she wasn't aiding in the commission of adultery.

Her nerves settled slightly, she slid her palm up his chest, his own heavy, hot one following suit. "I'm glad. I'd hate to think I was using borrowed goods."

He raised a dark eyebrow, intrigue reflected in his eyes. "That's what this weekend's about? You plan to use me, then toss me away like yesterday's news?"

Jesus, he made it sound so tawdry. Almost, as if he was offended by the idea. But that couldn't be. What man wouldn't revel in an offer like hers? "Is that a problem?"

He looked thoughtful for a long moment then grinned, the expression bordering on downright nefarious. "No. It's a proposition I'm very much gonna enjoy."

Nick lifted her hand from his chest, caught her first finger in his mouth and fondled the tip with his coarse tongue. His lips brushed back and forth erotically over her sensitive skin, his teeth nipping playfully at her damp flesh.

Stephie bit back a whimper. She had a dog that liked to suck on her fingers, but it never felt like this. So enthralling it shot to every single sexual crevice she possessed. She fought the urge to press her moist thighs together, or better yet sink them against his groin in search of his sex. If she did that he would know just how hot he was making her, and then she would never be able to convince him to leave this room.

"Follow me." He regained his hold on her hand, and with a yank brought her spinning around on the balls of her bare feet. For the first time she noted the other side of his bedroom. A small table and chair set took up the far corner of the room, the rest of the wall dominated by large windows and a sliding glass door that led out to a deck.

Joint forces of excitement and fear bubbled in her throat as he guided her through the door. A red-skied sunset enveloped her vision and balmy lake air allayed her senses as she stepped onto the deck.

"Oh, wow," she breathed. "What a beautiful night."

Less than a mile in the distance, an island dotted the evening horizon. Around them sea gulls and smaller birds swooped into the water. A brown-winged gull emerged from the surface, a fat fish in its beak, and squawked gaily over its catch. Several boats were visible from where they stood, but none so close that they could make out the occupants of the *Hidden Desire*.

Stephie let free a sigh. This place was perfect, their own little heaven on earth. Maybe she could give in to him here, relax enough to see if she'd been wrong about the whole control thing. Surely, it would be worth a try.

"I can't think of a better setting for dessert," Nick said, his tepid breath rolling along her neck. His hand came to rest at the small of her back and delicious waves of warmth spiraled through her already overheated body. "Can you?"

She left the sunset behind to meet his smoldering green gaze. He pulled her toward him, until their bodies were flush. The crisp hair of his legs rubbed against her calves, and his renewed hard-on pressed against the softness of her belly. She clamped her lips together to quell her moan of need.

Oh, God, could she really do this? Allow him to touch her without limits? Touching him was simple, gratifying. So long as her mouth was on him she remained in control. Nick didn't want her mouth on him this time around. The determined glint in his eyes ensured he wanted total and utter surrender, he wanted her to yield to him.

Her body tensed with the thought, and she knew no matter how badly she burned to feel him sliding inside her, strumming her ache with his long, slick shaft, she couldn't do it here, on his deck. At least, not this first time between them.

Somehow she had to lure him back to her room. "Nick, I—"

"Shh..." He placed a finger to her mouth to silence her. Rubbing the rough pad of his thumb over her lower lip, he backed her to a plastic chaise. He lowered her onto the reclining chair, then knelt in front of her and placed his big, strong hands on her thinly covered thighs. "My turn, sweetheart. Sit back and enjoy."

Panic reared its head as angry butterflies flitting through Stephie's belly, destroying the lust that burned hot in her womb. She couldn't just sit back and—

"Now what was it those dice said?" Nick rasped, bending his head in the direction of her lap. "Lick? Below the waist."

No! No, he wasn't going to—what the hell was he doing?

She arched her neck far enough forward to look down at him. His clever tongue ran over her Achilles tendon, evoking a tickling shudder along her calf. A laugh almost rolled from her mouth, but then halted as he nipped at her ankle.

A thousand sensations she never realized could be elicited by a bite in such a non-intimate place spirited up her leg and arced every hair on her body. She allowed her head to lull back, to surrender to the gentle balmy breeze whispering along her neck. He was teasing her feet after all, not her thighs, or somewhere far more arous—

Stephie jerked her head back up at the first stroke of his powerful tongue on the back of her knee. He was working his way up! Oh God, how high would he go?

All the way, dumbass. Remember, that's what you came here for?

All the way, he couldn't go all the way! But he was. Even as she thought it, his hands worked their way up her thighs and under the slits in her sheer gown. His large fingers kneaded her bared flesh with wondrous knowledge that no man had ever before shown her. Certainly not that first man seven years before, and definitely not Greg. He'd squeezed her knee a time or two, but that's as far as his handling went.

She liked Nick's brand of handling. She liked it very much.

As his mouth continued on its quest, his hands drifted ever higher, tracing the curves of her legs, her thighs, and then his deft fingers went even higher and glided over the edge of her swollen sex.

Stephie bit the inside of her cheek and whimpered at the heat of ecstasy crashing through her. She'd gotten herself off plenty of times, but never so easily. Never from a simple caress of fingertips over her clit. And she knew that's all it would take. A single touch of his finger and she would be floundering over the edge, hopelessly out of control. A marionette in his hands to torture or tease as it pleased him.

But no, she couldn't allow that. She couldn't be his puppet. Couldn't give in to the heady desire that swamped her, or the smell of her own sex that blended with the balmy night air. She had to fight this, to convince him to take this thing elsewhere.

Nick's rough voice cut through her thoughts. "Relax, sweetheart. Your toes are gonna curl right into themselves if you don't."

She couldn't. No matter how incredible his ministrations felt, she couldn't allow him to have his way with her, couldn't give in to the moistness that seeped from her parted thighs, making her ache to buck up and bury his finger deep into her heated core. She had to think. To remember why she must stay in control.

Remember how once he touched her, really touched her, he would forget all about pleasing her. He would forget everything but himself and his own needs. His gentle caresses would turn to cruel strokes, his grip would turn biting and he would thrust himself into her without a single care for her —

"Nick!" Stephie arched up as his thumbs jetted past her wet folds and circled the tiny nub that rested there, coming so close, but not nearly close enough to touching her puffed up, slick clit.

Tremors rushed through her as his sinuous strokes continued, tremors she longed to succumb to. Tremors that told her he wouldn't hurt her, he would make her feel the way a woman should. He could do that, she knew. And she wanted to let him. Right here on his platform deck with their own little bit of heaven surrounding them.

Nick couldn't stop from smiling at the sound of his name on her lips. He would make her cry out her ecstasy time and again, before they were through here tonight. He owed it to her for taking his pleasure first. He would never have done that had he known she'd go through on his dare. She had gone through with it. She'd gone down on him and brought him to soul-shattering climax, swallowed back his come as if it were the best thing she'd ever tasted. For that he owed her so much.

And, damn, how he ached to pay her back.

His fingers itched to bury into her shaved, damp pussy, again and again until she was creaming in his palm, but he refused to move so fast. He wanted to taste each delectable inch of her, rip her thin gown from her body, and spread the smooth folds of her cleft until her aroused nub was fully exposed to him.

His cock strained hard against his shorts with the need to grind into her tight, wet mound, and he pushed the edge of her dress higher on her thigh and bit at her silky flesh. She inhaled audibly, her fingers twining through his hair, as her breathing grew ragged. He nibbled higher on her salty skin, inhaling her female scent, the taste of her that would soon coat his tongue.

His shaft rigid and throbbing for release, he slid his fingers the length of her still clothed vulva and found her pulsating with the same need that licked hot as wildfire through every inch of his being. Still, he kept his fingers from the swollen pleasure point that lay in the middle of her sex, teasing the outer edges, rimming the sweaty, moistened folds, making them both mad with desire.

A helpless erotic sound broke past Stephie's lips, and she ground her nails into Nick's scalp and bucked up against his fingers. "Nick...please..."

He broke his hold on her inner thigh at the urgency in her voice, and looked up into her face. Her ruby red lips were puffed up just as he imagined her nether lips to be, and passion and need turned her eyes a mesmerizing shade of dark chocolate.

"Please what, Stephanie?" he asked, moving his thumb slowly, meticulously to the edge of her clitoris, and then rasping the rough pad of his thumb quickly across it. "What do you want from me, sweetheart?"

She shuddered beneath his touch, her eyes flew wide, and then she went completely still. Her hands fell from his hair to pound as fists on the chaise's seat. Eyes that an instant before had been riddled with passion turned hard as granite. Her mouth opened, and Nick knew from her expression her words would be anything but friendly.

"Get away from me," she bit out, pushing hard at his shoulders. "Get away from me, now!"

He stared at her angry, flushed face, and was lost in confusion. They'd been having fun, enjoying each other. What the fuck had he said or done to make her change her mind? "What do you mean, get away from you? What's the matter, Stephie?"

She shook her head. "Just...you...Damn it, Nick, just let me go."

Shit no. Not without an explanation. He grabbed her shoulders and narrowed his gaze. "Look, I'm sorry if I did something wrong, but whatever it was I'll make it—

"No! I said I want to go. Now let me!"

She pushed at him again, and he had no choice but to release her. He'd never held a woman against her will before and there was no way he would start today. Not even if the urge to push her back on the chair and torture her with his hands and mouth until she opened up to him ripped through every cell in his body.

Heaving a sigh, he rocked back on his heels and moved from her path. Stephie shot to her feet and dashed toward the sliding glass door. With a single parting glance, she disappeared out of sight.

Nick settled on the edge of the chaise and scrubbed his hand over his face. Why would she run away like that? Had she been angry, or was it another emotion that claimed her? Whatever her reason, her actions made no sense. Not when less than a half an hour before she was sucking on him for all she was worth.

"It makes no fucking sense," he vented to the lake in general.

Now what was he supposed to do?

Call your sister.

He should call and check on Emily and while he had her on the phone, have her remind him of what he was always reminding her. Nice guys don't sleep with complete strangers. That was the whole problem here. Of course, he couldn't know what was going through Stephie's head. They didn't know squat about each other. He knew she was a financial analyst and drove a Beemer and, oh yeah, wanted a sister, and had an ass to die for. In the grand scheme of things, that wasn't a whole hell of a lot.

He also knew she had a good sense of humor. At least, she seemed to have one those times when the tension between them died and they talked as normal human beings and not maniacs ruled by the baser need to screw like rabbits.

Christ, what the hell now?

What he should do is take a long cold shower, then dive headfirst into his work. Normally, he spent Friday night drafting ideas for the column due Monday morning. Only he knew himself too damned well. If he did that, he'd never get past word one. Not so long as there was an upset woman below deck. A woman he somehow managed to bring to near hysterics when all he'd meant to do was bring her to climax.

Real nice, Calanetti. Some bad boy you are.

Nick stood and started for his bedroom. He had to go after her and find out what went wrong. Two days was a very long time, as Stephie had pointed out more than once. Two days would feel even longer if he endured them without sleep, or worse, nights filled with her lusty body trailing through his dreams and making him hard as a rock even when she wasn't within sight.

Resigned to groveling if that's what it took to smooth things over between them, he started for the downstairs deck.

Stephie appeared at her cabin door the moment he knocked. Her eyes held a vacant edge, but other than that, she looked every bit as tasty as she had before she ran off. Which would have been a few short seconds before he uncovered her silky, shaved pussy and ate at her until come drenched his mouth.

Feeling his cock throb, he clamped down on the thought. He was here to apologize not fantasize. "Look, I'm sorry about...hell, I'm sorry about everything. I obviously got the wrong impression. But you gotta admit the way you were acting..."

She stepped closer and briefly touched his arm. "Don't apologize, Nick. It's my fault. You didn't do anything wrong. I just...you surprised me."

"I surprised you?" *Shit, that was a good one.* "You, sweetheart, shocked the fuck outta me. I never thought you'd actually go down on me like that."

Her eyebrows raised and a ghost of a smile played at her pouty red lips. The urge to lean forward and kiss her saucy mouth hit him full force.

"You didn't?" she asked.

Nick took a step back to fortify himself. Sleeping with a stranger was one thing, kissing a stranger was a whole other. A man could tell a lot about a woman by the way she kissed, and he wasn't sure how much more he wanted to know about Stephie. He already found himself liking her as a person, combined with the raging need to bang her pretty little brains out...well, one kiss and this thing between them could get messy.

"Hell, no," he admitted, hoping the truth would set his mind free. "I thought your bad girl attitude was an act—that you wanted to sleep with me to get even with Greg."

She looked utterly dazed then recovered with a rolling laugh. "Think again, Nick. This has nothing to do with Greg. I wanted you for you, not to get even."

"Then what happened?"

The amusement left her eyes, and she shrugged. "I got... Like I said, you just surprised me, I guess." Her smile growing, she stepped back and gestured toward the cabin. "I was about to put a movie in. Care to join me?"

"You're fuck..." No way would he say that again. If she responded with a teasing jest about him knowing when she was fucking him, he wouldn't be able to contain his groan. Let alone the way his penis thrummed when dirty words found their way into her mouth. "Do you really think that's a good idea? I mean, considering..."

She laughed again, this time the sound rang honest and clear. "It isn't a porno, Nick. I rented a couple of regular movies in case this weekend turned out to be a flop."

Not a porno. That was a good thing. At least he believed it was in some remote stretch of his mind. Some stretch that wasn't checking out the way her pearled nipples thrust against her nearly see-through dress all but begging him to lean down and have a taste of the full, tanned globes they crested.

"So, has it?" he asked, dragging his attention back to her face.

"Turned out to be a flop?"

He nodded, and she grabbed hold of his hand and pulled him toward the small sitting area that housed a carted T.V., DVD player and a generous selection of pornos. They reached the loveseat, and she turned to him. He was only half-surprised to see the eat-'em-alive smile had made its way back to her face. "There have been a few bumps here and there, but I wouldn't call it flop." She licked her lips and lowered her lashes coyly. "Besides, the night's still young."

Nick sank onto the plush leather loveseat and stared after her back as she went to the DVD player. The woman was going to drive him nuts with her conflicting moods. Five minutes ago she was demanding he let her go, and now she looked like she wanted him to hang on, to continue right where they left off. Damn, if that wasn't exactly what he wanted to do.

"So, what'll it be?" she asked. "Mystery or romance?"

"Comedy?" He could use a laugh about now. He could use anything that would take his mind off the constant ache in his shorts, and whether or not blondie was feeling up to extinguishing it again.

"Sure. I like to laugh as much as the next girl."

And she had a great one, Nick realized twenty minutes later, as they sat together on the small loveseat, the lights dimmed and the movie flickering on the television set. Just as he'd hoped, the film had lifted his brain from below his waist. What he hadn't planned on was the intimacy the darkened cabin lent. Or the way his mouth responded to Stephie's light, airy laugh. The smile that claimed him from the first soft peal had continually grown, rendering a carefree sensation he hadn't felt in ages.

As if she felt him watching her, she looked at him. "Not enjoying the movie?"

Yeah, but he was enjoying the company a whole lot more. She looked kissable in this light. Kissable in a soft way, not sexy or sinful. He reached a hand to her cheek and tucked a wayward strand of hair behind her ear. "I'm sorry about before. I just..."

"Forget about it, Nick. Like I said, it was my fault." Her mouth edged up to reveal her teeth. "In case you wondered, I was close."

"Close?" he asked, trailing his fingers along the smooth edge of her jaw line.

"To climaxing."

Oh, right. To climaxing. *Shit, so much for the magic of the moment.*

Nick pulled his hand back to his side and groaned. He was trying to make her see sex wasn't the only thing on his mind. That if she wasn't feeling up to it, they didn't have to do it. Apparently, sex was the only thing on her mind. And she was more than ready to partake in a round or two. "Stephie—"

She leaned nearer, her left breast brushing up against his side. "You know, if you really feel bad about earlier, Nick, there is a way you can make it up to me."

He frowned, doing his damnedest to ignore the play of her warm, lush chest on his body. "I thought you said it was *your* fault."

She turned to face him fully, and settled her soft, slender hand on his forearm. "Maybe I said that to make you feel better. So, do you want to know?"

He stared at her fingers on his arm, her bright red nails, then back at her face. Her lecherous smile told him whatever she was about to say wasn't going to be nice. It was going to be naughty. A naughty she'd go through with, or one she'd stopped the moment things started to get good? "All right, I'll bite. What do you have in mind?"

"Cuffs."

"Like hand cuffs?"

She nodded, her eyes gleaming with enthusiasm. "And ankle."

"Bondage? You want me to tie you down?" *Christ, talk about a fantasy come to life.*

Is that why she balked upstairs? She needed to be restrained in order not to run away? That was twisted. And kinky. And exciting as hell. "Am I misreading you?"

Her smile grew and amusement twinkled in her eyes. "Just a little. I don't want you to tie me down, Nick. *I* want to tie *you* down."

Chapter 6

Stephie nearly laughed out loud when Nick darted from the couch with lightning speed. He dragged his hand through his hair and looked back at her, his expression riddled with disbelief. "You want to *what*?"

"Cuff you to my bed, and..." *Say it, Stephie*, she ordered herself, feeling warmth rush into her cheeks. *He likes dirty talk. Just say the words and he's as good as yours.* She drew a shallow breath and squared her shoulders. "And fuck you."

The tic flirted to life in his jaw. Crossing his arms over his chest, he gulped and glanced around the dim cruiser's cabin, his gaze landing everywhere but on her.

He wasn't going to do it, she realized with a silent pout. Really, she couldn't blame him. They didn't know each other so well as to trust her to tie him up. Of course, lack of personal knowledge hadn't stopped her from performing a nosedive straight into his waiting lap.

That he allowed her to give him a blow job meant he trusted her a little. Surely, with a bit of encouragement that little would become a whole lot more.

Fortifying her bad girl courage, Stephie rose and crossed to where Nick stood near the television set. She laid her hand on his arm and tipped back her head, making him meet her eyes whether he wanted to or not. Indecision rested in his stormy green gaze.

She smiled with the realization he was tempted to do her bidding, just as she'd been tempted to do his back on his deck. She would have gone through with it, would have gladly melted into his arms, if only he hadn't called her by name — her real name.

The emergence of good girl Stephanie had dampened things between them in the short run. In the long run, however, her skittish bolt had worked out perfectly. By running away, she had lured Nick to her cabin, right where she wanted him.

She bit the inside of her cheek, recalling his sympathetic expression when he'd first appeared at her cabin door. She hadn't planned on seeing his compassionate side, or that he might apologize for something that was in no way his fault. If she'd caused him to worry over her, she'd do her damnedest to make it up to him. That is, right after she had him cuffed, stripped and moaning for release.

"Don't tell me the thought of bondage scares you, Nick," she said huskily, brushing her breasts over his crossed arms. His gaze narrowed and his penis stiffened, growing ever-so-slightly against her stomach, just enough to bolster her confidence. He would say 'yes' to her. It was simply a matter of persuasion.

She licked her lower lip and pried at his arms until he allowed them to fall at his sides. She moved closer, relishing the feel of his hard body pressed against her. "Or maybe it's the idea of a woman being in control that has you so nervous."

His lips quirked and the indecision in his eyes was replaced by humor. "Did I seem worried about control when you were giving me head? I can assure you, sweetheart, I wasn't the one calling the shots then."

Stephie grinned, knowing full well just how in control she'd been. In control, and loving every minute of it.

She pulled back far enough to splay her hands over Nick's wide chest. She'd felt the rigid planes of his body several times through his T-shirt, now she wanted to feel them free of the thin material, see his muscles bunched and glistening beneath her palms. His naked frame parallel to her own.

"You were a trooper," she conceded.

"And you have the tongue of Aphrodite."

He'd liked it then? Triumphant glee spirited through her, nearly making her giggle with excitement. Only Stephie's silent warning that bad girls didn't giggle kept the sound at bay. She couldn't contain the self-satisfied smile quite so easily. She really had no idea how one went about giving a blow job. She'd merely gone with instinct and did whatever came to her. Apparently, she'd done well.

Nick's appreciation for her actions chased away any insecurity that might have followed her down from his deck. Anticipation at what this night would bring had her heart beating fast, her body heating with moisture deep between her oversensitive thighs. Suddenly, even her light dress seemed stifling.

She slid her palms higher, eager to get on with the festivities, and have both of them naked and aching, to finally achieve the fulfillment she'd sought out for too many long, empty years. He would satisfy her several times this night, of that she had no doubt.

"I'm so glad you enjoyed your dinner fuck, captain," she purred. "Now, what do you say? Do I get to tie you down and lick you all over, or do we finish the movie?"

"Is it your fantasy?" he asked, his tone thick with desire, his erection full-blown and rock hard against the softness of her belly.

"To tie a man down?"

With a nod, he brought his large hands to her back and massaged. "Yeah."

She arched against his touch, wishing he'd bring his lightly callused fingers around to her breasts and fondle her tight, inflamed nipples through her dress. Or better yet coast them to the wetness that pooled at the junction of her legs, making her quiver for sweet release. "No. It's my obsession."

His fingers stilled. "You mean, I'm not the first?"

The burning need that whirled through her ebbed with his indiscernible tone. Damn, what was she supposed to say to that? Of course, he was the first man she'd ever asked to fulfill her bondage demand. But did he want to hear that she was so inexperienced she might as well be a virgin? It might be a turn on, or maybe a huge turn off. She didn't want to turn him off, she wanted him turned on so badly it was all he could do not to come the moment she allowed him entrance to her body.

"Let's just say I have a pretty good idea what I'm doing," she finally said.

He looked thoughtful for a long moment, then his skillful hands restarted their slow move over her back, teasing and taunting with their lightness when she knew how strong and powerful they could be if he chose. "If I agree, you'll let me go?"

Stephie's heart skidded into overdrive, and her smile grew to new heights. He was giving in! Hallelujah, she had arrived. Seven long years of waiting was about to reach its culmination. She'd never been more excited or deliciously terrified in her entire life.

"I will let you go" she breathed, feathering her hands past the rugged stubble that tinged the hard angles of his face, and into his hair. He had incredibly thick hair, black with cresting waves. Perfect for gripping as she rode him over the edge and into the throes of a mind-numbing orgasm. She eyed his neck and shivered at the thought of tasting his skin, of sucking at his flesh, and savoring his musky masculine scent. "Or I can keep you tied up until Sunday night, and use you at my will."

His eyes lit with interest. "And if you do that, will you feed me?"

She rose on tiptoe and twined her arms around his neck, seeking out the spot just below his ear. She needed that spot, needed it in her mouth, beneath her tongue, with a famished certainty. "What did you have in mind?"

"Something warm...and wet...and slippery." His smoky voice trailed near her ear, his hands skimmed down her back, evoking a tremble that momentarily splintered through her resolve to take his neck. And then it was all she could do not to lash out and sink her teeth into his tanned skin.

With effort, she curbed that urge and slowly drew her lips to his neck. She laved her tongue over his salty flesh, then blew on the dampness. He groaned and drew her closer, cupping her ass in his large hands until her breasts crushed against him and his erection rubbed invigoratingly against her moist, slick folds.

"Noodles?" she managed on a sigh.

"Uh uh. Try again."

"Hmm…warm and wet and slippery." Suckling at his neck, she skimmed her hands to the hem of his shirt and then beneath to scrape over the muscled sinew of his back. "God, you taste so good. Feel so good. I need more, Nick."

His fingers slid past the sheer fabric of her gown to stroke her naked feminine flesh from behind. "What about my food, Stephie?"

A ragged moan escaped her throat as he penetrated her with his finger, strumming the pad over her clit and stealing every ounce of strength that she possessed. Her legs shuddered and then gave way. He pulled her closer, holding her erect with one hand while he led her to a place that could be hell just as well as heaven for how sinfully incredible it felt. Sweat broke out on every inch of her body, and she lolled her head back, unable to think, unable to move. Unable to do anything but rock her hips against his palm and give in to the climactic tempo he'd set.

"Food, Stephie," he rasped, forcing her eyes open.

"Right. Warm, wet and slippery." There was definitely something warm, wet and slippery she wanted to get her mouth on and she had no idea how she'd been able to wait this long. Drawing strength from some unknown place, she moved her arms back to his neck and pulled herself to his lips. She needed to taste him, to kiss him, to pillage his senses as surely as she needed her next breath.

"How about tongue?" she whispered, then crushed her mouth to his.

For one extraordinary moment, Nick's lips moved, and her body hummed with the urgency she tasted there, then he went completely still. He set her back, righting her just when she thought her legs would give away and she would topple. She gazed at him, hope fluttering to the cabin floor like a gull with broken wings.

Why had he stopped?

Damn it, she'd wanted him, needed him, had to have him, and he'd stopped.

Before she could voice her thought, a wicked grin stole over his face and he took her hand in his own. "How about those cuffs?"

* * * * *

What the hell had he been thinking?

Nick stared down at the top of Stephie's head as she secured the last cuff in place around his ankle. He was trapped, tied down with no more than a pair of shorts covering him. No matter what she did to him, he wouldn't be able to stop her.

In and of itself that was pretty damned exciting, but when he thought about things, really thought, he realized how trusting it also was. He'd entrusted a near stranger to tie him to her bed and have her way with him.

And why? All because he'd been afraid of her kiss.

All right, he'd consider giving in to her before that, had a pretty good idea he was going to say yes when she'd rubbed her voluptuous breasts against him and eyed him with those big brown eyes. He'd been more than a little convinced he'd grant her free rein the moment he slipped his fingers into her wet, hot pussy and felt her body clench around him. Yet, until her lips brushed over his, he hadn't put voice to a response.

The instant her soft, pliant mouth settled on his, he knew he was in trouble. Scratch that, more trouble than what he'd already been in. She'd tasted warm and sweet and incredible. And like a woman he was dying to make his own.

That couldn't happen. At least she couldn't be his for any longer than this weekend. This weekend was about sex, about ending the long stint of tedium in his life. Not about finding the real Stephie — the intriguing woman who existed somewhere between the twin realms of good girl and bad girl she alternately showed him. This weekend was about gratification, a means to an end. A chance to get laid without having to worry over the repercussions. Just sex. Nothing more, or less.

Clearly, Stephie accepted this weekend for what it was. And this bondage stuff...well, hell, she'd as good as said she did it all the time.

He fisted his hands where they latched onto the bed frame. It shouldn't make a damn bit of difference to him that she did this on a routine basis, but it did. For a while back there, when she'd run from him in near hysterics, and as they had sat watching the movie and laughing like old friends, he had entertained the idea that everything occurring between them was as foreign to her as to him. That she was learning as she went as much as he was. Or rather making good on fantasies he'd only dreamt about in the past.

He'd been wrong in that notion.

Regardless of where she teetered on the good girl/bad girl front in all other facets of life, where men were concerned she was a tigress who delighted in controlling her lovers. He was her latest conquest, and it was high time he accepted that fact.

Finished with the cuffs, Stephie rocked back on her heels and raised her eyebrows in invitation. Her eyes gleamed with enthusiasm. She looked positively in heaven.

"Ready to rock, captain?"

As ready as he'd ever be to have sex with a woman who had no intention of ever seeing him again after Sunday night. That thought hadn't even crossed his mind when they'd been upstairs. Certainly not when her mouth was wrapped around him. He had to quit letting it bother him now. It was time for spontaneity, to throw caution to the wind and trudge on full speed ahead. His cock had a head start in that area. The moment she'd eased her body down his to restrain his legs, he'd become fully erect.

Ah fuck, who was he kidding? He'd become fully erect the moment she'd brought up the idea of bondage. This was a new game to him, but it was also one he couldn't deny the urge to play. Stephie might go through men as regularly as most people changed their underwear, but she was also alluring as hell. Tempting, teasing and designed to pleasure.

From her rolling laugh to her sumptuous body, he wanted her. Now if he could just keep her mouth from his, they could engage in the sort of mindless sex that seemed to be her forte. If she did try to get a kiss out of him...well, he'd cross that bridge when they came to it.

"What are you gonna do to me?" he asked, testing the cuff's strength.

Her lips curved in a secretive smile as she stood. "You'll see."

She darted from the bedroom, the hem of her short filmy dress fluttering behind her and showcasing her dynamite legs and rounded backside.

Nick bit back a grunt. Yeah, he'd see all right. Mindless sex or not, he couldn't wait to get started. Just too damned bad he wouldn't be able to partake in the activities the way he'd like to do, with his hands all over her supple curves, fondling her until she seeped with wetness. That time would come. As soon as she'd had her fill of the dominatrix role, he planned to have his turn playing the cuff-master.

A low, creaking noise reached his ears and Stephie reappeared, the wheeled cart that supported the T.V. and DVD player in tow.

"You plan to finish the movie?" He caught the disappointment in his tone and frowned. Hell, it wasn't his fault he was no longer in the mood for movies. He loved her laugh, but he also loved her ass. Not that he could exactly reach out and grab it.

Her eyes lit with amusement. "No. I plan to start a new one."

She lifted the thin, square case in her hand for him to see it was a porno. He stifled a groan as she bent before him, placing the silver disc into the DVD player. The plumpness of her bottom was outlined perfectly through her filmy dress, the cleft in her buttocks primed and ready for his enjoyment. It was all he could do not to tear his hands from the cuffs and fill them with her lusty ripeness.

She dimmed the lights to near blackness then sashayed to the side of the bed. The erotic sway of her full hips drew his attention to her pelvis and then to the center of her thighs. She'd been so wet for him when he'd stroked her moments before, moist, hot and needy. Would she slip onto him with a fast, hard thrust, or take her time, teasing and taunting him until he had no choice but to come wherever she wanted. Be it in her creamy white palm or hidden by the cotton material of his shorts.

"Do you like watching other people fuck, Nick?" she asked throatily as she sank down beside him on the big bed.

He swallowed hard, his shaft thrumming with her dirty talk. He'd never been much for pornos, but then he'd never watched one with Stephie. She had a way of making him want to explore previously uncharted waters.

"Do you?" he asked, as she crawled toward him in the center of the bed.

It was too dark to tell for certain, but Nick swore he saw color stain her cheeks just before she turned her attention on his torso. She trailed her long, sharp nails over his naked chest with a lightness that sent a shiver dashing through him.

A smile stole over her lips as she elicited another shudder. "I asked you first."

"I have a feeling I'm gonna enjoy this one." He had a feeling he was going to enjoy a whole hell of a lot where the two of them were concerned.

She drew up on her right elbow and brought her mouth to his chest. Her long, blond hair whispered over his skin, making him ache to run his fingers through the thick strands. Her tongue slipped between her parted lips and teased at his nipple. It pebbled beneath her warm, wet touch, and she moved to his other nipple and repeated the action. Her tongue swiped higher until it stroked a moist path along his neck, and he growled.

She peered at him, amused. "You're very sensitive, aren't you, Nick?"

He was responsive, yeah, but never like this, never where he felt he would come from barely more than a swipe. "I told you, you have a very talented tongue."

"Do you want to taste it?"

He shrank back on the bed, knowing damned well if she wanted to kiss him he wouldn't have a single choice but to allow it to happen. Christ, he wanted to, he ached to forage on her mouth. But he wouldn't do that, couldn't risk getting that close to her.

A keening moan followed by a second, more savage one, saved him from having to respond. They looked at the television screen at the same time. A generously endowed man rammed his bulging erection into a brunette's butt cheeks. The sound of flesh slapping against flesh mingled with their throaty cries.

Nick strained against his shorts with the need to get lost in Stephie's tight ass. He'd wanted to bury his cock in her backside since the moment he'd first seen her on the *Hidden Desire's* dock. He would before this weekend was over. First he wanted to sink into her tight, wet pussy.

A strangled sound escaped Stephie's mouth as she took in the movie. When she turned back it wasn't alarm that coated her features, but excitement. Passion rippled through her dark gaze and she licked her lips as if she couldn't wait to get started.

He mimicked that thought wholeheartedly.

"What do you say we lose a layer of clothing?" he asked as the couple in the background carried on with frantic huffs and puffs, and endless vocal demands.

Stephie sat back, straddling his waist and stared at the television set. She remained silent as the rise and fall of her chest increased and a tell-tale wetness damped his body where her thighs pressed against him. The man on the screen slammed into the woman one last time, and then came with a wild groan as he latched onto her hair. She cried out his name as he spilled his seed into her, and then hastily begged for more.

Stephie's crotch ground against Nick's throbbing erection as she looked back at him, and he bit back a pained grunt.

"It is hot in here, isn't it?" she asked softly.

Hell, yeah, and getting more so every second. Just as he'd guessed, watching pornos with her was the next best thing to making one of themselves.

The scene behind her changed to a woman cradled between two men, their sweaty, naked bodies joined and pumping in an offbeat pattern, but Stephie didn't turn back. Her clouded gaze remained constant on Nick's as her hands skated to the hem of her dress. The breath stilled in his throat, his balls drawing tight with expectation, as she lifted her hips up and inch by excruciating inch eased the sheer material higher

The hem of the gown came within centimeters of her creamy center and she let free the material to skim the fingers of her right hand to her crotch. "Did you like it when I stuck my fingers in my pussy and stroked myself for you, Nick?" she asked in a thick tone, her pupils dilated with her arousal. "I think you did."

Her fingers glided past the edge of her dress and then sank out of sight. Her eyes grew wider as she moved her hand up and down, slurping sounds erupting from her parted thighs, and hitching gasps tripping from her cherry red mouth.

Nick clenched his teeth, his cock burning with the desperate need to be inside her, filling her, making her climax with an intensity her fingers could never provide.

"Do you like this, Nick," she breathed, her words high-pitched as she moved faster against her palm. "Do you like it when I fuck myself?"

"Oh, yeah. I like it a whole lot." *Too goddamned much for sanity.*

He jerked on the handcuffs, tried twisting his wrists, then yanked on the cuffs again with all the frustration that raged through his body, but they refused to budge. *Sonofabitch.* He needed to be free, to get his hands on her, to kiss her. Damn his morality, but he had to sample her soft, lush mouth regardless of the outcome.

"Do you want me to come for you, Nick? Should I scream your name?"

He forgot about the cuffs with her needy cry, and nodded his response. That was definitely something he wanted to see, to hear his name on her lips, to watch the rapture play over her stunning face as she gave herself an orgasm. "Yes. Yes, that's what I want. Come for me, Stephie. Drench me with your juices, sweetheart."

Stephie slid her hand higher, the silhouette of her fingers beneath her dress clear as day from the glow of the television behind her. She arched her hips up as she drove farther into her body, then snagged her lip in her teeth and lowered her eyelids, rocking harder against her palm. The dress road up with her rhythm and finally Nick saw the shaved wet mound he'd touched twice already, but never long enough. And never when it wasn't masked from his view.

Jesus, she was beautiful, her muscles toned to perfection.

Two of her slender fingers drove in and out of her swollen vagina, her knuckles coasting repeatedly against her slick, fleshy folds. He held his breath in utter and complete amazement. With the exception of Stephie's small show earlier today, he'd never before seen a woman masturbate, seen her bury anything inside her other than his own shaft. Damn, he wanted to help her so badly, wanted to add his fingers to the array of glistening pink pussy and tanned skin.

Stephie's breath caught and she rode faster and harder. Sweat shimmered on her golden thighs and wetness lathered her feminine lips and the deep red head of her clitoris where she parted herself. Wetness gathered on the head of Nick's cock as well, staining his shorts and surging his testosterone.

"Oh, God, Nick, I can't wait any longer," she cried, tossing her head back.

She pulled her hand from her body, and then with a quick thrust, buried her fingers back inside and called out his name. She shuddered as come drenched her inner thighs and trailed down onto his pelvis, further dampening his shorts. Nick did the only thing he could and groaned with sheer wonder of how he'd ever been lucky enough to get to spend the weekend alone with Stephie and her naughty ways.

Her breathing still coming as ragged spasms, she tugged her dress up and over her head, tossing it away. Her full breasts jiggled, her nipples peaked and dusky pink, as she lowered herself to him and pinned his thighs between hers.

"You're exquisite, Stephie. Every single part of you is stunning." His hoarse tone conveyed the truth of his words, the reality of how badly he wanted her. If he could loosen a single cuff he would be inside her, ramming his cock into her tight lips and riding her until they were both too exhausted to move. But he couldn't loosen the cuffs and so he had to rely on words and hope to hell she'd offer him respite soon.

Meeting his eyes with a sultry smile, she brought the fingers she'd buried inside her to his lips. "Do you want to taste me, Nick?"

"Oh, yeah." *Taste her, touch her, inhale her one amazing inch at a time.*

She ran her finger over his mouth, the scent of her sex sweet and powerful as it infiltrated his nostrils and sent any supply of blood that still existed in his brain coursing to his balls. He parted his lips and took her into his mouth, suckled at her flesh until the last of her essence was gone and he could taste only her supple skin beneath his tongue. "You taste incredible, sweetheart. Next time you come. I want it to be in my mouth."

"I think I can do something about that." She rocked back, dragging her breasts with a tantalizing slowness down his chest, then moved up again, to the head of the bed, her moist feminine lips trailing a wet path in her wake.

Grabbing the bed frame, she lifted her body, and held herself just above his mouth. "Now what did those dice say? Oh, right. Lick, Nick."

Chapter 7

Nick gazed up at Stephie's swollen femininity, brilliant pink and glistening even in the dim light, and knew he was in heaven. She was fully exposed to him, her thighs spread wide, the cleft of her pussy parted just far enough to expose the nub cradled there. *Lick, Nick* — her throaty command brought a growl into his throat. She didn't have to say the words twice. He flicked his tongue out, over her silken folds, then buried it deep into her creamy center. She bucked against him, and he yanked on his wrist cuffs, yearning to be free so he could hold her in place while he ate at her.

"I'm not going anywhere," she promised in a husky voice, as if she knew his mind.

He probed his tongue deeper, savoring her heat, the musky smell of her that consumed him, the fact she trusted him enough to allow him to do this to her. "I love your scent, Stephie. I love licking your pussy and watching you squirm."

With a whimper, she bowed against his mouth. Before she could pull back, he reared up and caught her distended nub between his lips, suckled with brute force, then sent his teeth rasping over its entirety. Her breathing grew erratic, frantic gasps penetrated the near darkness as he continued with fast, furious rubs and sucks.

The blood hammering through Nick's body reached a crescendo as he worked his coarse tongue over her pulsating clitoris and tasted the urgency that rioted through her trembling limbs. The same urgency that had him burning for his own release. He would have his turn, right after he earned the right to hear her screaming his name.

He coaxed her harder, her tender flesh growing wetter and slicker with each deep, vibrant thrust. Her muscles shivered around his face, her gasps turned to intense pants, and then finally she clamped tight and convulsive around his tongue.

"Oh...oh my God. Oh, yes! Don't stop, Nick! Don't you dare stop!"

Stephie ground her soaking crotch against him, embedding herself again and again on his violently plunging tongue. Her juices streamed in thin drops over his lips, and into his mouth. Then, with a mindless scream, she coated his tongue with a waterfall of warm, sweet honey that nearly made him come as well.

With a contented sigh, she lifted herself free of his face and slid down from her position above him. A smile of fulfillment grazed her rosy red lips and her eyes all but blistered him with the heat of passion. She brushed a soft kiss over his mouth, and Nick froze, momentarily forgetting about his reckless urge to fuck her every which way but inside out. He'd said he wanted to kiss her, said he didn't care about the results, but now that she was kissing him...

Ah, fuck it. He had to do it for the sake of his sanity.

He raised his head to return the kiss, but before he could do anything more than rub his mouth against her pouty lower lip, she pulled away and moved down his body, her breasts and hair rubbing over his torso with teasing delight.

"You have way too much on, Nick," she purred.

Stephie dipped her fingers beneath the sides of his shorts, and he lifted his hips to help her remove them. She slid his shorts down as far as his widespread legs would allow and, meeting his eyes, cupped his long, thick member in the softness of her palm.

Burying her fingers in the hair surrounding his agonizingly tight balls and the base of his penis, she dropped her mouth to the engorged purple head and licked the moisture away. "I want to make you feel as good as you made me feel. Can I do that, Nick? Can I make you come for me and scream out my name?"

Could she ever. And if she kept up with the licking, damn soon. "I want to be inside you, Stephie. I want to feel it when you climax. I want you to feel me too."

Her eyes darkened further yet and she nodded. "I want that too, Nick."

"There's protection in the night stand drawer," he uttered, his heart accelerating to a lethal rate with the knowledge he would soon be within her slick, swollen pussy, grinding his erection to her core, feeling her come around him with intimate warmth.

Stephie sheathed him with trembling hands, the pressure of her fingers almost more than he could handle. She rubbed her drenched pussy against his burning erection, sending a million and one charges of need rushing through his body. He balled his hands into tight fists, when all he wanted to do was grab hold of her, thrust inside and carry her away on a thunderous wave of ecstasy neither would soon forget.

Grasping him in her hand, she guided him to the edge of her heat, then held him there, contemplation stealing over her face. "What's your last name, Nick?"

"Why?" he asked, genuinely surprised she cared. It wasn't as though she planned to see him again after this weekend. This thing between them was just sex — sex that would be over Sunday night. She didn't want anything more than that. Did she?

Had Greg been more to her than a weekend fling? Could she be the jilted lover using Nick for the sole purpose of revenge the way he'd once considered? Or maybe she wanted him for another reason altogether. Something more than just sex.

"We're about to fuck," Stephie cut in. "I thought it might be nice to know."

"Right." No. She didn't want anything more than sex. She wouldn't have spoken so harshly if that were the case. "It's Calanetti," he offered. "My father came over from Italy as a boy. My mother was dead set on making sure I knew how to cook Italian food." Why the hell had he told her that? Like she wanted to hear about his parents or his culinary skills at a time like this.

Her lips perked in a saucy smile. "You do your heritage proud, captain."

"What do you mean?"

She laughed and rubbed the head of his cock against her vulva, still not allowing him entrance, holding herself just above him. "Italian stallion."

Nick chuckled at the cliché. He'd had a past girlfriend or two comment on his size, but none of them had called him a stallion. He'd never felt like a stallion with them either. He felt like more than a prized breeder deep in rut with Stephie, he felt like a man who could do anything he wanted and more.

He focused on her desire swelled lips, realizing how badly he needed to kiss her. He couldn't sit up and take her mouth the way he was staked out, so instead he settled for a smile. "You're just too much, Stephanie Lang."

* * * * *

Stephanie?

Stephie stopped rubbing Nick's penis against her wet body and gaped at him. Why in the hell did he keep calling her that? Every time things started to get good, he would say that name, and make her second-guess her actions.

Not this time. Be she good girl Stephanie or bad girl Stephie, she was going to have Nick. She would show him the same pleasure he'd shown her, only not with her mouth but her body. The thought of feeling him explode inside her, sent a shiver of excitement coursing along her spine. She inched onto the straining head of his penis, just far enough to keep him with her without the need for holding.

The smile left his face and he groaned, the tic flitting at the corner of his strong, shadowed jaw. "I need more than that, sweetheart."

So did she. She needed to feel every inch of his masculinity impaling her—she no longer feared he wouldn't fit. As wet as she was, he'd slide right into her without a problem. Before that happened, she wanted to touch him, glide her palms over the impressive contours of his torso and down to the thick, springy black curls that surrounded his long, thick shaft. She yearned to feast on the spicy cavern of his mouth and feel his rough tongue mating with her own.

That is, if he would let her.

Both times she'd tried to kiss him he'd frozen. That last time after he'd gone still, he seemed to change his mind and decide a kiss was a good thing after all. She'd longed to see just how good of a thing they could ignite when their mouths melded, but she saw hesitation in his eyes. As if he were giving in against his will.

She didn't want a mercy kiss. She wanted one of complete agreement, of acceptance of how great they would be together. And they would be, somehow she just knew it. Their bodies were made to be joined, as were their mouths.

Her cheeks burned at the memory of Nick tonguing her slippery inner folds, and she was more than a little thankful for the low lighting. When he'd scraped his lightly bearded jaw over her clit and inhaled her scent, she couldn't hold back her ravished scream. No man had ever done that, buried his tongue between her nether lips and suckled at her as if she were his last meal. His fervent caresses had definitely been mind-blowing. And, as witnessed by the sticky moistness between her thighs and the endless heat that burned in her womb, more than a little orgasmic.

Still, it hadn't been real sex, lovemaking — or fucking as he chose to call it. Stephie bit the inside of her cheek at the less than ladylike term. Saying the word was one thing, but doing it, fucking someone was an action she'd never planned to take part in. It sounded too cold, too reserved. Nick was neither of those things. Nor was she. Any lingering doubt she'd had about their actions had long since passed. It was just the name for what they were doing that bothered her now.

Even that concern faded when she saw the savage hunger in Nick's sea green eyes. Between the appetite that waged there and the way his hands fisted at the headboard, she knew he was impatient for her. She was just as anxious for him.

Reclining forward, she splayed her hands over his hard body, her long nails nipping at the muscle and working through the light gathering of dark hair that lined his powerful chest. His bronzed skin stood out magnificently against the backdrop of the black silk sheets. His arms corded where they stretched to the handcuffs, his thighs spreadeagled and rock solid beneath her.

He looked every bit the Adonis she'd first pegged him. And maybe even better. "This is going to sound tacky, but you have a beautiful body, Nick."

He raised an eyebrow. "You don't strike me as the type to worry over tact."

He was absolutely right. Bad girl Stephie didn't give two shits about tact, or how the outside world perceived her behavior. Bad girl Stephie only cared about one thing. Having her fill of the man splayed beneath her.

"You're right, Nick." She eased herself back to a sitting position and slowly allowed his bulging penis to slip into her, inch after impressive inch. "I don't...care." The last word came out on a choked sigh as he slid almost completely into her, filling and expanding muscles that hadn't been occupied by anything more substantial than a vibrator for seven long years.

"Goddamn, Stephie," he growled. "You're so tight, sweetheart."

She gripped his hips, digging her nails into his taut flesh, and closed her eyes. She *was* tight. Tighter than she'd ever imagined. Her breath caught as he sank the remainder of the way in. She stiffened and her eyes watered with pain. He was too big for her. Son of a bitch. Everything had seemed so perfect. They'd developed the basis for a wonderful and exciting friendship, and he was too damned big for her.

If they continued this, carried out their mutual cravings, he would only hurt her more than what he had, and she couldn't allow that. No, she wouldn't allow that. She'd promised herself years ago no man would ever cause her physical pain again. It didn't matter if the man in question was harming her on purpose or accidentally.

Nick lifted his hips, the ridges of his erect shaft stroking the sensitive skin of her vagina. An unexpected rush of sensual warmth teased through her, soundlessly beckoning her to forget her past and the fears that racked through her, tightening her body past the point of pleasure. If she could just forget, just concentrate on the here and now and that he didn't want to hurt her, maybe this would be okay. Maybe.

"I want to touch you." His raw voice abraded her panic, soothing the edges of her frayed tension. "I want to put my fingers between us and stroke you, but I can't. You have to move, Stephie. Move against me, or pet yourself. Just don't go on hurting."

Stephie snapped open her eyes and gaped at him. He looked worried, his forehead knit and his expression a mixture of concern and unbridled lust. The concern turned her stomach with guilt and had her biting down hard on the inside of her cheek. He knew he'd hurt her. What's more, he was trying to make it better. Damn it, nothing about this night was going the way she'd planned. She was supposed to be calling the shots, ruling him, not allowing him to guide her and tell her how to turn the pain to pleasure.

Still, she did as he suggested and holding tight to his hips, arched against him, rocking her body so that his hardened shaft moved inside her. She closed her eyes again, half-expecting the hurt to continue or possibly to worsen. Instead, the pain died and the promised pleasure flowed through every crevice of her being, restoring the heat of desire and sending warmth sliding through her veins hot and heavy as liquid silver.

"Open your eyes, sweetheart," Nick pleaded, his voice rough. "I want to know you're thinking of me when you come."

She opened her eyes and laughed softly, white lightning arcing through her with delectable force, rendering her limbs all but weightless. How could he believe she'd want to think of anyone else? And who would that someone else be? Greg? Hardly. If it were Greg with her now, she would still be in pain, she would continue to be in pain until the heinous act—and it would have been heinous had she given herself to that two-timing sleaze-ball—was finished.

Nick wasn't Greg. Nick sure as hell wasn't like that other man all those years ago.

Nick was compassionate, and considerate, and if she'd come onboard the *Hidden Desire* to find a man for the long-run and not just one to indulge her fantasies for the weekend, he would be just what she was looking for.

"Stephie," he ordered, his brow creased, "stop thinking. Just feel."

She caught her lower lip in her teeth and nodded mutely. He was right. No thinking. Only feeling. Giving into the bone-melting sensations he stirred.

She lowered herself to him, her sensitized nipples scraping over his hair-roughened chest and further stimulating the heady need coursing through her. She wanted to hold his hands, to seek comfort in his strength, but that would mean letting him go, and she couldn't, not just yet. Settling, she grasped his forearms.

"That's it, Stephie. Hold onto me," he encouraged. And then he started to move.

She hadn't realized he was holding back until right that moment. And she didn't think on it for another second as all her thoughts centered on maintaining her grip on his strong arms as the rest of her ascended to a magical place where she felt as light as a bird and twice as capable of spreading her wings and soaring.

"Nick!" The word tore from her lips as the orgasm shook her body, shuddering through her limbs and turning her vision to a blind haze.

"I'm right with you, sweetheart. I'm right there."

And he was. The explosive tremors that shook his big body racked through her, spurring forth yet another mesmerizing climax.

Nick's thrusts came to a halt, and Stephie collapsed against him, her energy spent and her body humming. Her head on his warm chest, she listened to his heart leaping as they fought to regain normal breathing.

"That was..." beyond words. Beyond anything she could imagine.

"Incredible," he supplied. The word was labored and yet she heard the satisfaction there, the appreciation for just how good they'd been together.

She smiled against his chest. "Incredible, and then some."

Several minutes passed before Stephie had enough strength to lift her head and meet Nick's gaze. He looked satisfied, as she'd guessed he would by his voice, and maybe a tad cocky. She felt a bit cocky herself. But more than that she felt sure of herself, more aware of her sexuality than she'd ever before even considered.

Bondage had been an excellent idea. She could look her fill, revel in Nick's magnificence, and then take him with the knowledge she was in complete and total control. At least, nearly in total control. For a moment there, as they ascended toward a mutual wave of pleasure, neither of them had been in control.

Too bad the fun was over.

But it had to be. Nick had trusted her to tie him up, and she owed it to him now to let him free. And then what would happen? Would he hold her, spoon her, the way she'd often heard her friends' lovers and spouses doing after sex? Or considering he called the lovemaking they'd just taken part in fucking, would he think his job here was done, and get up and leave without another word?

Unsure which she preferred, him staying or leaving, Stephie unhooked the wrist cuffs. She eased down his body to the ankle cuffs, already missing the feel of him inside her, the hasty beat of his heart against hers, the mixed scent of sex and sweat.

The moment the last cuff let free, Nick caught her from behind and pulled her up against him. His brawny arm wrapped around her middle and her heart swelled at the sense of completion that washed over her. Whether they were weekend lovers, or something even better, he was a man she would never forget.

"Thanks for letting me go," he said, placing a soft kiss near her ear.

Emotion gathered in her throat with his gentle touch, and she nodded her reply for fear if she voiced it, more than a simple 'you're welcome' would come out.

His hold on her tightened then, his arm continuing to constrict around her, until she wondered how tight it would get, or if he planned to squash her altogether.

The answer came in a way she never could have anticipated.

With one fluid move, he spun her onto her stomach and drew her arms over her head, securing her wrists with the cuffs. Stephie's eyes flew wide and the breath snagged in her throat, bile rising up as blind fear overtook her.

Oh, dear God, no! He wouldn't. But he was. Her gentle, compassionate Nick was taking control. She bucked against him, a wild scream erupting from her mouth.

He shackled her ankles as if she lay still, then leaned down and whispered in her ear, "Your turn, sweetheart."

Chapter 8

Covering Stephie's body with his own, Nick brushed her golden hair away from her nape and dropped his mouth to her neck. The smell of sex had begun to fade and in its place was the jasmine she'd spritzed on her body earlier that night. He licked at her sweaty, sun-kissed skin, savoring the way she trembled in response, her whole body racking from his touch.

She'd said he was sensitive. Judging by her frantic wriggling and increased breathing, she was more sensitive than he could ever imagine being.

He swept her hair further to the side, exposing her left ear lobe. Sending his hands over her bare sides, he nipped at her delicate flesh, suckling at the pulse point just below her ear. She squirmed beneath him, her body arching up, and stoking to life a fire he couldn't seem to keep vanquished around her. She squirmed a second time and his quickly returning erection cradled in the seam of her ass, expanding like clockwork and bringing his thoughts back to the porno that sounded behind them. He'd been so wrapped up in Stephie, he'd forgotten the television was even on.

Continuing to tease her silky smooth skin with his rough hands, Nick glanced at the screen where a woman was secured to the ground with ropes and stakes, and two men were alternately sticking their cocks in her mouth and pussy.

He scowled at the scene. He didn't want to watch that, he wanted to rewind to the moment when the man had taken the woman from behind. The same moment when Stephie had looked at him, her face glowing with excitement and her breath coming out as ragged spasms. She'd looked anxious to attempt the kinky sex portrayed on the screen. He was more than eager to lose himself in her firm buttocks.

His pulse sped with the thought her backside would be every bit as tight as her front. Her lips had been so taut, her muscles so compact around him. He'd taken a virgin once, long ago. She'd felt like that woman had, only a whole hell of a lot better.

Stephie wasn't a virgin, of course. She was the wanton wonder of all his wet dreams. And for this weekend, she was his.

Nick returned to his position just below her ear and nuzzled away the hair that had found its way back to cover the object of his attention. Stephie released a soft cry, and tried to block the onslaught of his mouth by craning her head against her shoulder.

He chuckled at her wasted attempts and pushed his way back to her neck, resumed his feasting. He could kiss and lick and suck at her satiny skin for hours without getting bored, cradle her sumptuous curves in his arms for nights without growing weary of the feel of them, of her delicious scent swirling through his nostrils. He could, anyway, if this thing between them was about more than sex.

It was really too bad she didn't want more. They got along well, seemed to enjoy each other's company and humor. They definitely appreciated each other's bodies. But as Stephie had told him upstairs, she wanted to use him for the weekend and then walk away. She didn't want a commitment, a lasting relationship. She just wanted sex.

If she was only his for the weekend, then he'd be damned sure when she left him on Sunday night, it would be with a smile on her face and his memory firmly etched in her mind. He would be the seducer that knew no bounds, the playboy she craved.

His blood pumped harder with the thought of sliding into her perky little ass, ravishing her with nothing but carnal satisfaction on his mind. He raised his mouth to rim her ear. "I saw your excitement when we watched those people fuck. Your eyes were shimmering. Did you like seeing the man enter the woman from behind, or was it that you hoped I would do the same to you?"

A strangled cry drifted up to him. He reached his hand beneath her and filled his palm with a generous breast, treasuring its weight and suppleness. Her breathing grew louder as he stroked her nipple, fondling its tips with the pad of his thumb until it grew hard, and a barely audible moan escaped her lips, followed by, "No."

He laughed at the word, knowing by its throaty ring she didn't mean stop, but continue. He pulled his hand from her breast and moved it between them to run down the rolling curves of her backside and skim over the rear of her sex. She shuddered when he glided the tip of his finger into her body then went stiff beneath him.

Nick frowned at her rigidity. More so, the lack of moisture at the cleft of her parted thighs. She was slightly damp, but not like she'd been moments before. To be fair, she had come several times already. Maybe her body had run out of its day's supply of lubricant— if such a thing was even possible. More likely, she was sore from when he'd first entered her and caught the etchings of pain shimmer over her beautiful face. If she was tender, then the last thing he wanted to do was make her ache worse.

But what if she wasn't sore? What if she was playing hard to get. The confident sex-goddess who'd taunted her way into his pants would pull something like that. If that was her game and he let her go, he wasn't liable to get his turn as cuff-master again. No way in hell would he give that fantasy-laden role away so easily.

"What do you say, sweetheart?" he asked, dipping his fingers deeper into her pussy, petting her mound in an attempt to restore her wetness. "Do you want me to stick my cock in your ass?"

"I...no. Let me go."

Anger edged into her voice, and he jerked his hand from her body. Rising to straddle her thighs, he scowled at the back of her head. What the hell was her deal? Just like on his deck, the moment he tried to take her over the edge, her moans of pleasure turned to those of annoyance, and she acted like...

Holy shit, she acted like a nice girl!

A girl who was afraid of trying things out of the ordinary, of being fully exposed on a deck viewable by passersby, of being cuffed to a bed and taken from behind.

That logic fit, but it still didn't explain her treatment of him. She'd tied him to her bed without a second thought, masturbated in front of him until she climaxed, then cried out her bliss when she came in his mouth. Nice girls didn't do that kind of stuff.

Well, what the fuck was the matter with her then?

Greg. The obvious answer hit him square between the eyes. She felt guilty because she'd slept with Nick to get even with her ex. Was the man even her ex? Stephie had claimed the two of them were through. Had she lied? That had to be it. They'd fought, and she'd run away and sought comfort in the arms of another.

The fact he was that other man knotted his stomach, but Nick refused to voice his frustration. She was already upset enough for both of them. The last thing she needed was for him to blow his top. "It's okay, Stephie. Greg doesn't have to know about this. No one has to know but you and me."

"Greg?" Confusion sounded in her voice. "This has nothing to do with Greg. He was a sleaze-ball, and I'm through with him."

And he believed her. Something in her tone ensured her words rang true. But if Greg wasn't the reason for her behavior, then what? Could it be fear? Was she feeling the same things he felt? The beginnings of attachment, of wanting to be with him longer than this weekend, and she was dealing with it by turning away?

He lowered next to her on the bed and cupped the side of her face, the urge to kiss her pouty lips and set her worries to rest, stronger than anything he could remember experiencing. "Does what's happening between us scare you, Stephie?"

She shook her head, a bare whisper of sound as her hair brushed over the silk encased pillow. "No." She jutted out her chin. "I'm not scared."

"Well, if you're not scared, then what the hell's the—" He stopped short and looked away, needing to regroup, to remember the temper that threatened was based on frustration and not anger.

His gaze landed on the cuffs that secured her slim wrists in place and realization dawned as vivid as the morning sun on the open water. He looked back at her, noting the worry lines that creased her forehead. "It's the cuffs, isn't it? They frighten you."

Incredulity coated her gaze. She retorted with a vehement, "No."

"Yes. They do."

She thrashed her head against the pillow. "They don't, Nick. It was my idea to tie you up. Why would I start something I didn't want to finish?"

He smiled at her bravado, not believing her words for a minute. She'd started this bondage game because she never planned on the table's turning—that he would want to have a turn as the controller. Had he known how it would affect her, he likely would never have taken one. But now that he had, he had to see it through.

Nick ran his hand down her back, over the swell of her plump ass and fingered the silky smoothness of her crack. "All right, Stephie. You're not scared, you don't have a problem with what's happening between us, then relax and let me make love to you."

Her eyes flew wide. "What?"

He ran his finger over the seam of her bottom once more then sank it between her firm cheeks. His cock hardened when her anus tightened around him. "Let me take you like this," he breathed in a gruff whisper, raising his free hand to fondle her breasts, "with your wrists and ankles shackled and your legs spread for my pleasure."

He drove his finger deeper and Stephie's whole body shuddered. A shaky sigh broke her lips. "Please. Nick..."

"Please what, Stephie? Do you want me to stop?"

She was quiet for so long that he nearly pulled his finger back out, but then she spoke, her words almost inaudible, yet filled with undeniable hunger. "No. I want you to continue. I want...I want you to take me like this."

Nick growled at her response, his sanity all but snapping at the thought of riding her this way, taking her from behind. "Are you sure?"

God, yes, Stephie was sure. She'd never been so sure of anything in her life, and that truth was beyond astounding. She should be frightened right now, deathly afraid of the things he could do to her when he had her pinned this way, things another man had done to her, but she wasn't. All she felt as his lightly callused finger slid along the crevice of her bottom were shivers of ecstasy charging through her body.

His rough palm worked each of her breasts in turn, plucking and rolling her stiff nipples, warming her from deep within. She didn't feel out of control now, or scared as was her initial reaction, she felt wanted.

And, oh, how she wanted in return. "I want this. I want you, Nick. I want you to touch me. I want you to drive me wild with your hands, your mouth, your tongue. Make me break free of these chains. Make me lose control."

"Ah, sweetheart, I thought you'd never ask."

A wicked grin formed on his mouth just before he rolled to the side of the bed and yanked open the nightstand drawer. She bit back her whimper at the loss of contact. He would be back. He'd continued his finger's quest and follow it up with the rest of his body, until he was impaled in her. She shivered involuntarily. She would not allow fear to reenter her mind. There was nothing to be afraid of. It was just Nick, and for the most part she could see what he was doing.

Leaving the nightstand drawer ajar, he moved to a sitting position, his back against the big bed's headboard and his shaft standing proud and firm between his legs.

He smiled mischievously. "Close your eyes."

"*What?*"

He held up a black silk mask. "Close your eyes so I can put this on you."

Stephie bit back a denial. Still, it rang loud and clear in her mind, rekindling her apprehension and tensing her muscles. To enjoy his skilled touch, the foreign heat that surged through her when he held her captive was one thing, but to do so blindfolded, when she had no idea what he was doing to her body —

"You're not scared, are you, Stephie?"

His voice sounded mocking, as if he thought her behavior was all part of the game. It was, at least it should be. It had to be. If she were ever to break free of the bonds that held her captive, not those on her wrists and ankles but those buried deep in her heart, she needed to succumb to him completely.

Fortifying her courage, she flashed an openmouthed smile. "The only thing that scares me is the thought you'll put that on me and leave."

His eyes shimmered with excitement as he bent to her mouth and teased a kiss at each corner, his rough stubble arousing in its contrast to his soft lips. "Trust me, sweetheart, I'm not going anywhere."

Neither was she, not when his mouth was so close to hers, almost as if he wanted to kiss her. Not out of obligation, but because the need churned within him as wholly as it did within her.

She could do this, she realized with a definitive certainty. She could do anything so long as Nick was her partner. "Then let the games begin."

Nick slipped the mask into place, and blackness enveloped Stephie's world, shrouding her sense of sight and sending that of smell, sound and touch to new heights. She acclimated to the sound of their breathing, hers heavy and his shallow, to their mixed scents, hers light and floral, his stronger and purely male, and with it came the tinge of panic. She held her breath, urging the sensation to pass. Warm fingers stroked over her nape and her nerves turned from frazzled to energized as minuscule hairs stood on end.

His rough knuckles grazed her flesh as he freed her hair from beneath the mask's elastic band. He lifted the heavy strands away, and her stomach tightened as his sensuous mouth found her skin. With his tongue, he trailed wet kisses over her neck, the velvet stroke slightly rough and incredibly arousing then he worked his way down her back, his hands never moving past her hair.

This is what she'd been afraid of? These light, teasing touches that were slowly building an inferno low in her belly? Well, hell, if she knew this was all that she had to fear she would have given in to another man long before this. And that was pure bullshit. She knew better than to think all men would handle her so gently. There was a reason she'd waited as long as she had. She'd been waiting for Nick, even if she'd only known he existed somewhere in the farthest recesses of her subconscious.

She relaxed against the silk sheets, allowing his tender caresses to lull her into a mindless state. "That feels good," she whispered huskily as he pressed damp kisses to the small of her back.

"I know something that will feel even better," he promised, pulling his mouth away. The bed swayed with his weight as he moved from her body, then the mattress righted again telling her he had risen. His footfalls retreated against the carpet, and she choked back the urge to call his name. He said he wouldn't leave her, so he had to be coming back.

Less than a minute later, the footfalls came again, the bed creaked gently and coarse leg hair rubbed against her skin. Hard muscles settled around her back and hot thighs pressed against the top of her own. An unmistakable granite hard erection rested along her buttocks. Stephie sighed her relief, relaxing anew. He'd come back.

An object light and unfamiliar settled on her forearm then slowly coasted downward, dancing along the flesh of her arm, stimulating in its weightlessness.

"What do you feel?" he asked.

"I don't know. Soft?"

He eased the device across her back and slowly down the length of her spine, into the hollow just above her buttocks. "What else?"

"Light."

The object coasted further down, until it brushed over the crack of her ass. What felt to be a hundred tiny pricks of energy glided back and forth, up and down. The unfamiliarity of the device made the sensations all the more intense. "And now?"

"Ohhh...good." She tightened her cheeks instinctively, her stomach a mass of raw nerves as she eagerly awaited his next move.

Nick chuckled lightly, then moved the object lower still, down between her widespread legs where wetness pooled in abundance. What felt to be countless tiny heads rimmed the edge of her slick vulva with a wicked lightness she shouldn't have felt at all, but felt in every inch of her body. Shards of hungry need sent her blood boiling and she reared back against the exquisite touch, her shackles binding her from any real movement.

"More," she demanded in a needy voice she barely recognized as her own.

"Not until I'm ready." He teased her with the nameless object, tracing the edge of her swollen sex again and again, the many soft edges skittering back and forth against her quivering clit. She bowed up and fisted her hands at the headboard to keep from climaxing against the deliciously subtle caress.

"Do you like that, Stephie?" he demanded, cupping her left butt cheek in his large, callused hand and fingering the swell.

"Yes!" she cried out. His rough fingers moved in time with the nameless object, petting her ass while the toy petted her exposed, wet mound. "Yes, I like it."

"Then give in," he ordered gruffly. "Don't be afraid."

"I'm not afraid!" Son of a bitch. Why did he insist on coming back to that? She wasn't afraid, not at all. She was waiting to feel him inside her, thrusting deep into her buttocks, before giving in to the powerful orgasm that tugged at her from every angle.

Both the object and his hand left her body, and she whimpered. "Don't stop, Nick."

"Not on your life."

He'd barely completed the sentence when something small and hard entered her, probing against her swollen, wet lips, teasingly erotic with its anonymity. The object drove in and out, brushing again and again over her aching clit. She fisted her hands in the cuffs and squeezed the muscles of her vagina, attempting to sink it further into her, to end the mad need that spiraled through her, soaking her body with sweat and her thighs with her own hot juice, whether he was inside her or not.

"Do you want more, Stephie?" he growled.

"Yes! More now!" She reared back again, seeking out the device, struggling to break free of her bonds. To her horror he pulled the object away. "Nick!"

"Patience, sweetheart," he murmured, amusement clear in his tone. He gripped her left butt cheek almost painfully. "Here it comes again. Tell me if you don't like it."

"I'll like it!" she barked hoarsely. "Just put it back in."

He didn't bother to mask his humor this time, but let out a rumbling laugh that shook from his body and into hers. "Your wish is my command."

The device came again, but bigger, broader, and more intense. The pricks she'd felt on her ass scraped at the folds of her feminine flesh, coiling explosive heat in her belly and endless wetness at her junction. "Oh my God. What is that?"

"Do you like it?"

"Yes," she bit out on a moan, as the heads moved faster and harder, stroking her incessantly. "I've never felt anything…it feels incredible, Nick."

He chuckled once more then took it deeper. "It's your hairbrush."

She almost exploded with the admission. Her sexual threshold pushed to its limit with the idea something so archaic could cause such pleasure. *"My what?"*

"Your hairbrush," he repeated, still fondling her with the kinky toy. "I can tell how much you like all those little heads rubbing over your pussy. You're so wet, sweetheart. I wish you could see the juices leaking down your thighs, the way your clitoris is pulsating. You can smell it though. Do you smell your sex, Stephie? Musky and warm? It makes me want to eat you out all over again."

"Yeah. I mean…" What the hell possessed him to stick a brush up her with all the toys this place had to offer? Screw it. Who gave a shit what his motivation was just so long as he kept going. "I can smell it, Nick. It makes me want to taste myself. I wish I could see what you're seeing, lick the juices from my thighs."

"What do you want me to do with the brush, Stephie?"

Never in her life had she been so excited and deliciously terrified by a response as the one she was about to give. "Fuck me, Nick. Fuck me hard."

A groan left him as he rumbled, "With pleasure."

He buried the brush deeper, massaging the bristled ends over her clit, eliciting moans from deep within her throat and shudders throughout her body. She was so close. One more rub and it would be all over, nothing left to her but a puddle of a sweat and a thoroughly satisfied smile.

Nick's weight lifted from her body and his coarse leg hair rasped over her calves as he moved downward. His lengthy, erect penis thrummed against her thigh, further firing a need that already burnt out of control. Once more the brush left her, and Stephie cried out in angry protest. "Damn it, no! I want more!"

Without responding, he cupped her bottom with both his large hands and kneaded her sensitized flesh. "I love your ass, Stephie. All you have to do is turn around and I get hard. I love sticking my fingers in you." He glided his thumbs to her inner cheeks and parted her. She forgot all about the brush and trembled at the idea he was looking at her so intimately, in a place not even she could see without the aid of a mirror.

His next words, peppered with a husk that ensured he truly did love what he saw, turned her trembles from those of apprehension to those of pure excitement. "You make me so hot," he murmured, strumming her ass crack with his big, rough fingers. "I don't want to waste you on this brush. But I will. Because I know you want it, and because I want to watch you. There's nothing better than watching a woman come, listening to her cry out her rapture. I want you to cry out for me, sweetheart. Scream your ecstasy. Will you do that?"

"Yes. I'll do that for you, Nick. I'll do anything." She would do anything, try anything he wanted, because she knew now beyond a doubt that he wouldn't hurt her.

He drew his fingers free of her and ran the beaded head of the brush along the swell of her bottom once more, then removed it from her body as well. Still she could feel the cool edge so near to her sex she trembled from its almost touch. The wetness between her widespread thighs grew heavier, more pungent with her anticipation. The air around them was colored completely with her scent now, balmy and near to stifling.

Needing release more than she needed her next breath, Stephie bucked up in search of the brush. "Now, Nick," she begged shamelessly. "Fuck me now. Please."

"Like this," he asked, resting his hand upon the back of her thigh. The tip of brush stroked against her clit and she moaned long and loud.

"More?"

"Oh God. Don't tease, you idiot. You know I want more."

He chuckled softly. "Teasing is half the fun, Stephie."

Nick moved the brush further into her, the head sinking into the folds of her drenched vagina and sending a ripple of raw desire straight to her toes. He moved his hand from her thigh and eased two callused fingers into her buttocks. Brush and fingers buried deeper, thrusting into her in turn, and she cried out at the sheer delight of feeling both sides of her sex being stroked at once.

The rhythm of the brush grew, as did that of his fingers, both slightly rough as they rammed into her, both more arousing than anything she'd ever known. Her breathing grew intense, the air jerking from her lungs in almost painful spasms. Yet she could hear Nick's breathing, erratic and harsh as her own, and she knew he was nearly as close to coming as she was. Only she was just a bit closer. An earthquake started deep within, shaking her with a soul-shattering need to let go, to give into the orgasm brought about by the best sex toy she'd ever had the pleasure of experiencing.

Her toes curled, her thighs trembled, and as the come drained from her body, soaking everything in its path, she knew two things. She would never again look upon her brush without reverence and, just this moment, at the hands of Nick Calanetti, she'd found liberation from the shadows of her past, the fulfillment she'd always dreamed of, the deliverance she knew existed somewhere for her.

And sadly it wasn't enough. She wanted, correction, needed more. She needed Nick — her Mr. Right.

"I want you now, Nick. I want you inside me."

Chapter 9

Nick sank against Stephie's back, gathering her in his arms as he caught his breath. He'd never witnessed anything more erotic than watching her bare pussy spewing forth around her hairbrush. Using the brush on her sure as hell hadn't been his intention when he'd gone to the bathroom. He'd wanted lubricant to ensure that when he entered her she wouldn't experience pain, as she'd seemed to the first time. Then the brush caught his attention from the sink basin, and he'd forgotten all about lubricant.

As exciting as the idea of running it over her tight, lithe body had been to him, he hadn't expected her to get off on it so completely. She had gotten off, a whole hell of a lot judging by the wetness of the bed and her current gasping struggle for air.

Sometime in the last half hour or so, she'd also gotten over her fear of attachment, or whatever it was that had kept her from giving into him. For that he couldn't be happier, because if he didn't penetrate her soon, he was liable to make the bed an even wetter, stickier mess than it already was.

"Enter me, Nick," Stephie pleaded hoarsely beneath him. "Take me like this. Stick your cock in my ass just like we watched that man do to that woman."

His balls tightened painfully with her words, and he bit back a guttural groan. He'd kill to do just that, enter her tight ass and ram away until her cheeks were filled with his come, only he didn't think he could. Rather he wouldn't make it all the way in before he went off. Tonight he'd settle for entering her slippery, hot pussy from behind. Tomorrow, though, was a whole new day.

Wanting her coherent in every way when he entered her, he came up on his knees and removed her mask. Stephie turned her head and their eyes met. She flicked her tongue over her passion-reddened lips and dropped her gaze to his mouth. Her voice came out a lusty whisper. "Let me in, Nick. I want to taste you."

He nodded his assent. He wanted that too. He'd wanted it long before this, and now that the time was here, no way in hell would he turn her down. "Yes."

Sliding his hands down the curve of her spine to the small of her back, he parted her lips and sought out her tongue. She met him halfway, stroking with fervor, with urgency. She increased the pressure, mating with his mouth in a hard fast dance, then pulled back and thrust in and out erotically.

He groaned at the sinuous swipe of velvet over his lips, and the careful control he'd managed the entire time he was pleasuring her, withered away. His shaft thrummed with the need to be inside her. Making her his if only for the weekend.

Desperation urging him on, he broke free of her mouth and settled himself over her. He edged her parted thighs wider yet, then filled his hands with her lush, sweaty breasts, and sank his teeth into the smooth, damp skin at the back of her neck.

"Yes, now! Take me now!" she cried on a labored breath.

Aligning his cock with her soaking cleft, he roughly plucked and twisted her stiff, burning nipples. Blood hammered lethally through him, sending a roaring to life in his ears. "I want to come in your ass, sweetheart. I've never wanted to do that to another woman, but I've wanted to do it to you since we met. Only I can't. I'm too damned hard, and you're too damned tight. This time I come in your sweet, little pussy."

Even as the words left his mouth, he drew back and pierced her hot womb. She cried out her encouragement as he thrust into her again and again, working her nipples harder in his callused hands, biting and sucking at her tender, salty neck. Nick growled his contentment as Stephie's breath caught on a ragged gasp and her body tightened around him. She tipped her hips and rocked, doubling the tempo he'd set and tightening Nick's testicles until he thought they would burst.

Knowing he wouldn't last much longer at this intense rhythm, he pulled his hands from her breasts and entwined them with her cuffed ones at the head of bed. He sought out her lips, shivering when she met him openmouthed and flicked her tongue against his. This is how he wanted them to be, joined completely, mouths, hands, and bodies when they climaxed.

Stephie's breathing grew stronger against his mouth, her heart drumming in the same reckless manner as his own. He took over the kiss, much as he took over their pace, coaxing her with his body, his mouth, the play of his fingers. She tightened around him, trembling delectably, and he groaned deep in his throat. The trembles turned to quakes, and then massive waves that crashed through her and tugged at him.

"Come with me, Nick," she wailed as the muscles of her vulva strained impossibly tight around him. "I want to go together. I want to feel you with me."

Her body gave one more fierce pull, and he tumbled over the edge and into the throes of his own soul-branding orgasm. His breath and heart stilled for a violent instant as sensation after sensation pooled through him, rendering him numb, weak. Immobile. Then he was gasping for air, struggling to breathe at a rate that didn't defy the threshold of space and time.

Stephie went limp beneath him, and it was all Nick could do from falling onto her and crushing her with his weight. Drawing strength from an unknown reserve, he came up on his knees and freed her from her bonds. He fell back onto the bed, his energy spent. With a throaty sigh of contentment, she curled up in his arms and rested her head on his sweaty chest. For a long moment neither said a word, then in a soft, sleepy voice, she murmured, "That was perfect, Nick. Thank you."

He smiled down at the top of her silken head, still not sure he could breathe well enough to say more than a word or two at a time, yet more than sure he should be the one doing the thanking here. "No. Thank you," he managed.

She yawned and snuggled closer, threading her slender fingers through the dark curls on his chest. The silence of a few seconds ago returned, this time lasting much longer. Once again she broke the stillness. "Are you close with your parents?"

Nick jerked at both the sound of her voice and the surprising question. He thought she'd fallen asleep, or at least was lost in satisfied musings. He'd have never guessed in a million years her thoughts had drifted to his family. Why had they? What possible reason could she have for wanting to know about his parents? Whatever her motive her voice sounded genuinely interested.

"I was...they died," he finally admitted, part of him hoping she wouldn't ask anything further, part of him praying she would. It had been too damned long since he spoke about his parents to anyone other than his sister. Whether it was from the intimacy they'd just shared or another reason completely, he found he wanted to tell Stephie about them.

"I'm so sorry." She placed a kiss on his chest, then again cradled her cheek against him. "I don't know what I'd do without my parents."

"Mom and Dad died in a plane crash a few years ago," he offered without further encouragement. "They were coming back from Sarasota in a small charter plane. The authorities still aren't one hundred percent clear on what happened, but they blamed the crash on engine failure." His voice shook with the painful memory of receiving that late night call. He forced the too vivid recollection free of his mind. "Anyway, my sister took it pretty hard. I think that's why she acts the way she does. She can be pretty wild at times."

What was Emily doing now? Nick couldn't help but wonder. That was the biggest pitfall of his weekend job. As much as he enjoyed the time away from his often nonsensical younger sister, he also spent it worrying over her safety. That concern would be expanded considerably if his career choices took him away for more than just the weekend but for whole weeks at a time.

"You said you didn't like that age—nineteen. What was it like for you?" he asked, hoping Stephie could set his mind at ease.

She stiffened in his arms, the idle rubbing of her fingernails over his chest ceased. "Nineteen was awful," she said passively. "That was the year I learned about control."

He frowned at her unexpected response, the indifference of her tone and how falsely it rang. "What do you mean," he asked, wishing she would look up at him so he could see her expression, "learned about control? What kind of control."

"The only kind," she responded in the same flat tone, still keeping her face averted, her body too tense to be comfortable. "I hate being out of control, Nick," she admitted. "I never allow myself to get that way, which is why I panicked at first when you cuffed me to the bed. But I changed my mind, because I trust you."

Sonofabitch. So she had been afraid. And what had he done to soothe her, but use a goddamned brush on her. But damn it, she'd said she liked it. She'd encouraged him.

"You never allow yourself to get that way?" he prompted, desperately needing to hear the rest of her story, why she felt the way she did, and if she truly had enjoyed the sex they just shared or merely pretended to for his benefit.

Stephie nodded mutely, her long, blond tresses bristling over his naked flesh, shimmering vividly in comparison to his black chest hair. "No. I never give away control. I have to be the one calling the shots. I *had* to be the one calling the shots," she amended. "I don't feel that way with you. I feel powerful with you, strong regardless of who's in control."

Nick's guilt settled with her words. Still..."But why? What are you afraid of?"

She lifted her head, her chin digging into his chest and her normally expressive eyes eerily vacant. "The only other time I let someone else have control, he hurt me."

The guilt he'd felt returned in spades, and his gut churned with dread for the words she was about to speak. He tightened his hold on her, hoping and praying he was wrong. Still he couldn't keep the quaver from his voice. "He hurt you? How did he hurt you, sweetheart?"

The slightest touch of emotion passed through her deep brown gaze, then again the dull vacancy reclaimed it. "In the worst way he could have. He raped me, but—"

"No way," Nick gasped, the churning turned to an all out burn, "you're not—"

"Yes. It happened. But it was a long time ago, and I've moved past it. I just haven't given away control since then. Not until tonight."

Holy shit, how could this be happening? How could he, a self-proclaimed nice guy, have handled her so crudely? He should've taken things slow, taken the time to kiss her, caress her the way he wanted to do, to savor each inch of her beautiful body. "When? I know you said when you were nineteen, but when did it happen? How?"

She shrugged, as if it were no big deal. "On a blind date. One thing led to another and then when I said no, he wouldn't stop. He…he slapped me, then laughed when I cried." Long-buried hurt entered her voice, her eyes growing bright with tears he knew she wouldn't dare shed in front of him. She shook the emotions away and smiled. "Like I said it was a long time ago, Nick. I've dealt with it."

Dealt with it maybe, but never again allowed herself the freedom of unbounded sexual exploration before tonight. "Why me? Why of all the men you could have would you choose a stranger to finally let loose with?"

Stephie returned her cheek to his chest and splayed her hand over his heart. "You're not a stranger, Nick. Maybe we don't know each other a lot, but we know enough. And well," she added lightly, "maybe just because it was time. I can't very well spend the rest of my life tying men up, now can I?"

He waited for her to say more, something that didn't sound so flippant and completely detached from her true feelings, but she didn't make a sound. Seconds turned to a full minute still she remained silent, motionless aside from the steady rise and fall of her body with her breathing. He rubbed her back soothingly, longing to say something but feeling inept and, worse, like a complete asshole.

Goddamn his stupidity! He was endlessly telling Emily about the bad guys of the world. The one's who were after her solely for a quick fuck. In the space of the last few hours, he'd all but become one of those bad guys. He'd damned near hurt Stephie in a way she couldn't forgive. Never again would he allow his dick to rule his brain.

Whether she believed it or not, Stephie was a nice girl, and it was high time she was treated like a lady. It was well past time that he remembered he was a gentleman.

Nick opened his mouth to voice that exact thought when her soft snore reached him. He closed his mouth and frowned. Was the sound any more authentic than her nonchalance toward the rape? Her sleep very well could be real. With the emotional highs and lows she'd faced in the last few hours, coupled with a generous dose of sex, she was likely exhausted. Regardless which claimed her, exhaustion or denial, the time had come for him to leave.

Stephie had given him a treasure tonight, one he would always hold sacred, but she hadn't offered anything outside that, hadn't asked him to stay the night. Most importantly, she hadn't said one word about feelings, or that she thought something could be happening between them other than chemistry.

The truth was black and white and, for reasons beyond him, hurt like hell to accept. Stephie had come to him for the express purpose of sex. While that sex had become more elemental than pure physical need, they were still almost strangers, and the odds were good that when this weekend ended it would be with them parting ways forever.

* * * * *

Stephanie woke with a smile on her face and the sultry feel of silk gliding over her naked, sweaty limbs. She reached to the bed beside her, longing to feel Nick's strong body, to indulge in the sensual lovemaking he'd shown her the night before. Only this time slower. She wanted to remember every move, every moan, everything to the expression on his face when he climaxed. Or better yet, when they came together.

Her hand kept reaching without coming into contact with a warm, virile male body. She opened her eyes, lifted her head and gasped. He was gone!

Of course he's gone, dumbass. Last night was about sex. Did you really think he'd be here come morning?

Great. Worse than Nick being gone, bad girl Stephie had returned.

Stephie was right of course. Last night had been about sex. That she felt they'd connected on some intimate level, enough to share the hurtful secrets of their past—his about his parents' death and hers about the rape—was clearly just her imagination.

Besides, it wasn't as if she didn't know where he was. They were on a forty-foot pleasure cruiser in the middle of Lake Michigan. If she wanted to see him, all she had to do was knock on his cabin door.

She did want to see him. Badly. Really badly.

It wasn't healthy to feel so dependent on a person you barely knew. But then as she pointed out to him last night, they really weren't strangers. She knew things about him. She knew he was considerate and a gentleman when it mattered most, that he loved his sister enough to spend his weekend worrying over her, that his parents had been killed in a plane crash. And that he would never hurt her. Never raise his hand to her or touch her in a way she wasn't comfortable with.

Still, that wasn't enough. Those were only facts. They didn't tell how he felt about her as a person, if he felt anything at all. Maybe he did. Maybe he felt the same gentle stirrings of attachment that warmed her heart. How would she ever find out one way or the other? She couldn't very well ask and risk him saying 'no'. Not unless she wanted to spend the rest of this weekend holed up in the cabin watching movies and playing with sex toys that no longer appealed to her unless Nick was on the other end.

She'd read, Stephanie decided, sliding from beneath the cool sheets. Read and lay out in the sun this morning. Then later today, if he hadn't come to her yet, she would go to him, and see how things stood between them—if he was interested in continuing what they'd started, or if last night had been a one time deal.

* * * * *

Sonofabitch! He couldn't get any damned work done.

Nick had sat at the small table in his room, laptop burning bright for hours last night attempting to draft his column for Monday's paper, and all he had managed to type was 'The'. Ten years he'd been writing the local news syndicate column and all he could come up with was a single syllable.

Real fucking great.

Sinking down in his seat at the small table, he scrubbed his hand over his face and struggled to get his thoughts away from the previous night and on his job. That proved near impossible considering he'd woken with a hard-on and semi-damp bed. He was too damned old to be having wet dreams. Tell that to his penis. More importantly, tell that to his brain, the one responsible for rendering up that picture perfect fantasy of taking Stephie from behind, one hand filled with her breasts and the other stroking her wet pussy.

Christ, it had been so damned erotic. And so wrong.

After what she revealed to him last night, Stephie deserved gentle sex, soft words and softer hands. Not him ramming his cock in her ass. What the hell was wrong with him that he couldn't erase the sinful urge from his mind? As he'd told Stephie, he'd never wanted to do that to another woman. What was it about her? All she had to do was turn her back to him, wiggle her bottom and, whether he'd just had her five seconds before or not at all, he wanted to mount her like a dog in heat.

"Nick."

He bolted up in his seat at the sound of her voice behind him. Shit, how long had she been in the room and was there any way she could know the direction of his thoughts? He hoped to God not. She needed time to think, to see if things looked different in the light of day, not pick up on his restless need to taste the unknown.

"Stephie. Did you sleep well?" he asked, swiveling in his seat.

Nick's gaze landed on her tight black tank top and the generous swell of cleavage thrusting against the lacy vee, and his erection went on full alert. He took in the rest of her clothes—khaki shorts and sling-back sandals—then returned to her bountiful chest.

"I slept like a baby," she said softly, "but I've actually been up for hours."

He pulled his attention to her face and frowned. "Hours? What time is it?"

She smiled and walked to him. His heart beat harder with every step. Then nearly catapulted out of his chest when she placed her hand on his shoulder and bent down to tease a soft kiss over his lips. "A little after one."

His thoughts jerked from her actions to her words. "Ah, Christ, your lunch. I'm sorry." Some kind of host he was. Last night he didn't let her eat more than five bites and today he was starving her.

She wove the tips of her long, red nails over his shoulder and along the edge of his back, reminding him too well just how damned good they'd felt biting into his flesh. "No big deal." Her smile grew until her pouty lips curved upward in a way that looked an awful lot like naughty. "I mean, yes, I'm hungry. It's just that…well, I thought you might be hungry too."

He gulped down a breath. "Are we talking about food?"

With a sultry laugh, Stephie dropped onto the edge of the table, her hip rubbing against his laptop. She leaned toward him and cupped his face in her hands, licked her lips. "I was thinking more like breaking in that lounge chair on the deck."

"You, ah, wanna make love out there?" Dear God, could a man get any more excited than he was at this moment?

She leaned closer still, until her breasts brushed against him and her lips feathered along his ear. "No, Nick. I want to fuck out there."

"*Excuse me?*" What was she talking about? She needed to go slow, to do things the normal way. She deserved that much. Why the hell didn't she realize that?

She drew back and reached into the dip at the front of her shirt. Gold glinted in the sunlight that bled through the windows and sliding glass door. Nick realized the glimmer was the necklace she'd worn upon her arrival at the resort at the precise moment she revealed its decoration—a cross.

Holy shit, she was religious!

Her lips edged up further into that eat-'em-alive smile he'd come to know so well. She brought the small 'T' to her mouth and ran the long stem over her pouty lower lip. "I was thinking we could do that thing we never got around to last night."

"Th-that thing?" he choked out.

She sucked the end of the cross between her lips, the sound too close to the one elicited by her fingers when she slid them into her wet pussy. "You know, the thing about sticking your cock in my ass."

Chapter 10

Stephie caught the heat in Nick's eyes and knew just how badly he wanted to agree to her offer. She'd spent the morning blissfully remembering last night, praying he was doing the same. For a long while, she'd held out hope he would join her on the deck, or better yet ask her to come back to his bedroom. He hadn't done either, and she'd grown tired of waiting, wondering if he regretted their actions.

Smiling down at him now, she knew he had no regrets, only confusion. His bewilderment was justified. Until he'd held her in his arms and showed her just how incredible losing control could feel, she never would've considered granting his fantasy of taking her from behind. But he had held her, kissed her, chased away her fears. And now the idea of anal sex was more exhilarating than she ever imagined possible.

Letting the cross fall against her chest, she rose from the table and lifted her eyebrows in invitation. "So, what do you say, captain? Are you up for it?"

His gaze narrowed, he pushed his chair back. "Why do you wanna do it?"

"It's your fantasy."

"It isn't yours." He shook his head and frowned. "I told you last night, I've never had a woman like that. I could hurt you, Stephie. I won't risk it."

Her smile grew with his concern for her welfare. The reason he wouldn't risk it, was exactly the reason she'd let him do it. He was compassionate, genuine, the only man she would trust to do something like she was suggesting.

She caressed his shadowed jaw. "You won't hurt me, Nick. You couldn't."

"How can you be so sure?"

Because he'd told her so himself, but that wasn't the reason she believed him. After all, another man had spoken those same words to her and they'd turned out to be a horrific lie, one that cost her seven long years of sexual freedom. Nick was so much different than that other man. The truth was in the way he touched her, kissed her, the unwavering compassion in his sea green gaze — almost as if he cared for her.

A shiver of excitement stole through her with the thought. She bit down on the inside of her cheek and forced it away. She'd promised herself today wouldn't be about the way he felt toward her, but the way he made her feel. Tomorrow would be another story. Though the last thing she'd come on this boat to find was a relationship, she couldn't help but wish when they docked tomorrow night, it would be with them exchanging phone numbers if not house keys.

"You were gentle with me last night."

Nick snorted. "Which time would that be, when I was fisting my hands in your hair and coming in your mouth, or when I was shackling you to the bed and cramming a brush up your pussy?"

The smile left Stephie's face at his gruff self-accusation. She moved between his thighs, savoring the feel of his crisp leg hair rubbing against her smooth skin. She caught his stubbled chin in her hand and ran her thumb over his sensuous lower lip.

"I loved every moment of both those things, and you know that's not what I mean," she said softly, mesmerized by the texture of his lips, the strong contour of his jaw, the tang of his masculine scent. "I trust you, Nick. And I want to make your fantasy come true, just like you made mine."

His gaze went leery, and he captured her wrist in his hand and drew her thumb from his mouth. "What do you mean, I made your fantasy come true? I thought you said you never wanted to give in to control in the past. How can that be your fantasy?"

"I was talking about bondage."

A frown deepened the corners of his lips, disbelief colored his words. "I thought that was your obsession, that you'd done it a number of times."

The air stilled in Stephie's throat as she realized her mistake. She'd made him think she was a tried and true veteran of the bondage game, that she was more than capable of controlling a man. And clearly that's what Nick wanted to believe. He wouldn't be scowling if the idea she'd been a first time participant pleased him. And that could only mean one thing, he didn't give a rat's ass about her beyond sex.

If he cared about her at all, he'd be exuberant to know she hadn't been around the bondage block. Or any other block for that matter.

She pasted a smile on her face, while her heart pressed with ache over her foolish notion he could want something more from her. "I'd never done it with you."

"Oh." His frown faded and he let go of her wrist. He stood and closed his laptop, placed it on the cubbyhole shelf over his bed, then turned back. "If you want to make love, I'd be more than happy to join you, but I won't fuck you."

Stephie fisted her hands at her sides, her thoughts and emotions in a quandary. He didn't care about her, yet he wouldn't fuck her. That made no sense. Unless, she'd been wrong and he did care. But if that were the case, then why was he happy to think she'd been with so many other men?

"I don't understand," she admitted. "Why are you willing to make love to me, but you won't fuck me? And what difference does it make what we call it? It's just sex either way, right?"

Nick glanced away and dragged his hand through his hair. "Yeah, I guess so."

But he didn't sound like he believed it. He looked almost appalled by the idea she could put two very different words into one grouping. In reality, she didn't believe they were the same either, that anything that had happened between the two of them was just sex. There was much more to it than that.

If he believed that too, what would it take to get him to admit it?

She crossed the room and laid her hand on his chest, stared up into his turbulent eyes. "I'm asking you to have sex with me, Nick, just the way we did last night. I want to feel you inside me. You make me feel strong, powerful. You make me unafraid to lose control." She took his hands in hers and brought them to her breasts, squeezed until her nipples pushed achingly at his palms and heat pooled deep in her loins. "I want you to touch me, to kiss me. And then when I'm ready, I want you to enter me."

She rose on tiptoe and, pinning their hands between their bodies, took his mouth in a long drugging kiss that spoke of need and desire and the secrets of her heart. "Please say 'yes'," she breathed against his warm mouth. "I need you so bad."

Releasing a loud sigh, he pulled his hands from between them and brought them around her, holding her close. "You make it so hard to say 'no'."

She tipped back her head, certain her happiness showed in her eyes. He cared for her. Maybe not in a huge way, but she knew deep in her heart he cared a little, enough to fear hurting her. Enough that when this weekend ended he might want to continue what they'd begun. "Then don't, Nick. Let me make your fantasy come true."

He nodded and brushed his lips over hers. "All right, sweetheart. You win."

* * * * *

Nick concentrated on Stephie's back as she pulled him through the sliding glass door to the deck. He wanted to look lower, wanted to feast his gaze on the swell of her plump ass, but he was already having enough trouble dealing with the fact she wanted him in it. Damn, he didn't want to hurt her. And he feared he would. She might act like a confident bad girl unafraid to ask for what she wanted, but he knew where the levels of her confidence lay and he also knew she wasn't a bad girl.

It had taken all his self-control and more not to shout out his happiness when she accidentally revealed she'd never lived out her fantasy of tying a man up before last night. She'd tried to cover her blunder, and refusing to hurt her feelings he'd gone along with it, but he didn't believe her words for a minute.

As happy as the truth made him, it also worried him. She said she'd never had sex with a man when he wasn't bound, but if she'd never before bound a man, then she also hadn't had sex with one in years. Not since that horrible day when she was assaulted. He still couldn't figure out why she'd picked him to end her celibacy streak—her answer of 'it's just time' wasn't cutting it. It also couldn't be that she felt anything for him. If she did, she would've never called what they were doing fucking.

Stephie sat on the end of the lounge chair and tugged on his hand. "Come here, big boy," she purred, as she laid back. "I'm ready for my lunch."

Nick allowed her to pull him down, so that he straddled her thighs. Even as her lips found his, his thoughts returned to the previous night, to how tight she'd been when he entered her. She'd felt like a virgin. And maybe for all intents and purposes she had been. Brutality didn't count as sex. It sure as hell didn't count as lovemaking.

Christ, how could he go through with this knowing how inexperienced she was, of the way he'd already taken her so cruelly, with an object no one in their right mind would think to use as a sex toy. Stephie deserved weeks, if not months of tender passion before they advanced to this level.

"Nick, honey, what's the matter?" she asked, caressing his cheek.

He froze and stared into her deep brown eyes. *Honey?* Had she just called him honey? That was a pretty damned intimate term for someone she wanted to spend the weekend fucking, then send on their merry way. Unless, she didn't want to be rid of him so soon. Or maybe not at all.

Clinging to that hope, he smiled. "Nothing. I was thinking."

She slid her hands down his back, bunching the material of his shirt to expose his torso to the summer sun. "Someone once told me not to think, just feel."

She grated her nails over his bare muscles and, unable to deny the carnal need her touch spiraled, he growled deep in his throat. "Hmm...I think I can handle that."

"I know I can," she responded in a lusty whisper, then again found his lips.

This time Nick's thoughts didn't voyage beyond the heated cavern of her mouth. He drank her in with his tongue, his lips, as his hands slid between their bodies and skimmed over her soft curves. He cupped the lushness of her breasts through her thin tank top, then roughly worked his thumbs over her nipples, groaning when they beaded with expectancy.

Stephie broke free of his mouth and tugged at the back of his shirt. "Off."

He chuckled heartily as he drew up on his knees and pulled his shirt over his head. Her hands quickly found their way to his chest, her fingers running over his muscles, through fine, dark hair, and down along the ridges of his abdomen.

She leaned forward and licked at his flat nipples, caught one in her mouth and grated the tender edges with her teeth. Raw desire churned every particle in his body, and his shaft grew taut against the brush of her thighs.

Stephie didn't miss his heated response. She dropped her hand to his shorts and slid it past the elastic waistband to cup his erection. She ran her fingers over his ridged length, squeezing and stroking him until he grunted from the bittersweet agony.

God, she drove him wild with her unabashed handling. "I can't get enough of you, Stephie. Can you feel how hard I am for you? How bad I want to come in your hand. Just a touch and you make me wanna explode."

Her pouty red lips drew up in a smile and her eyes shimmered with dazzling emotion. "You take my breath away, captain."

She removed her hand from his shorts and tugged her tank top over her head to reveal a lacy black bra that might as well have been made of air for all that it covered.

Nick stared at her dark areolas through the filmy material, her nipples erect and straining, and he released a guttural groan. "I'd say you do a pretty damned good job of breath-stealing yourself, sweetheart."

"You're not the only one who wants to come right now, Nick. My nipples are burning for your touch. Can you see how hard they are? They want your mouth on them. The rest of my body wants you too. My pussy wants your fingers buried in it. And do you know what my ass wants, Nick? My ass wants all of you."

Her and her dirty talk. Now that he knew just how inexperienced she was, it was all the more effective. His balls tightened and his fingers itched to dig into her soft mound, to slide into her and coax her into an orgasm. His cock throbbed most of all.

He bent his head and took her erect nipple in his mouth, suckling at her though the thin material, reveling in the way she wriggled against him. Gliding his palm down her flat stomach, he loosened the button on her shorts then eased down the zipper. His fingers stroked over the cotton covering her sex, already soaked with her essence.

"Yes, Nick," she cried, her fingernails biting into his back. "Bury them inside of me. I need you inside of me."

His fingers went under the edge of her panties and fondled her moist, swollen lips. She squirmed against his hand, demanding more with her mouth, her body. He bit down harder on her nipple and gave into her plea, penetrating her with two fingers.

"Is this what you want, Stephie?" he rasped, stroking this thumb over her clitoris as he continually thrust his fingers into her body.

She trembled in his arms, and he knew she wasn't far from coming. He wanted her good and wet, soaking enough to lubricate both sides. "Oh, God, yes. I want that."

"You're close, sweetheart. Your pussy's clamping around my fingers. Can you come for me, fill my hand up with your sweet taste?"

"Yes. Yes, I want to do that. I want to come in your hand."

Cradling the back of her head in his left hand, Nick lengthened the rhythm of his right, burrowing deeper into her, petting her ripe, juicy body, coaxing her muscles to give in to his caress. She gripped his fingers with a sudden powerful force, and digging her nails deeper into his back, showered him with her nectar.

"Oh, God, Nick. I'm coming! I'm coming!"

He grinned at her hoarse scream. Yeah, she most definitely was coming, and everyone on the lake knew about it.

Stephie bowed against his hand, drenching his palm, the inside of her silky thighs and the crotch of her panties and shorts, then finally went slack, resting her head against his shoulder. Her breathing grew more normal, and he knew the time had come. If he was going to enter her from behind, he had to do so now when she was still dripping wet and, judging by the way her lips quivered around his fingers, not far off from another climax.

He sought out her mouth, needing to taste her one last time before he turned her over. She shook away from his kiss and stared to somewhere in the distance. "What are you doing, sweetheart?"

She nodded. "There's a boat over there. Can they see us?"

Nick glanced to the boat where two people were positioned at the bow, then back at Stephie. "If they have binoculars, they can see every move we make."

Her eyes went wide. "Do you think they do?"

"Yeah," he admitted. "The boaters around here know this stretch of lake's the *Hidden Desire's*. They know what happens on this boat."

Stephie shivered, her body contracting around his fingers. He groaned inwardly. The last thing he wanted to do was take the time to go elsewhere. She would never stay wet enough, not to mention his resolve to follow through with this would die. Still, he wouldn't make her do something she was uncomfortable with. He would never do that to her, especially not now that he knew her past.

"Do you wanna go inside, to my bedroom?" he asked.

A slow smile claimed her lips, breaking out into a much bigger, more devious grin. "No, I want to give them something to talk about."

Nick felt her body contract around his fingers again, the added wetness that pooled between her thighs, and he realized that she wasn't upset but excited. He grinned at her naughty response, ceaselessly astonished by the way she surprised him. Just when he thought he was getting a glimpse in to her personality, she said or did something to totally throw him off kilter. This kind of off kilter he was all for.

He grinned. "It arouses you to think they're watching us, doesn't it?"

"Doesn't it you?"

"*You* arouse me." And amazed him. And so very much more.

He took her mouth in a thorough, bruising kiss, strumming her moist folds for several more seconds, then pulled his fingers from her body and eased off the lounge chair. She looked up at him expectantly, waiting for him to make the next move.

"Roll over, and drop your drawers," he said in a gentle, yet commanding tone.

"Yes, sir, captain," she quipped, then promptly did as he asked, dropping her shorts and a sodden scrap of black that could only be her panties into a pile near her feet. She bent in front of him and reclined on her stomach at the edge of the lounge chair, laid her palms flat on its seat, and wiggled her ass.

Nick moaned loud and long.

Stephie laughed. "Does that mean you like what you see?"

All but licking his lips at the sight before him, he kicked off his shorts and donned the condom he'd slipped into his pocket this morning just in case it might come in handy. Lowering to his knees, he cupped her firm butt cheeks and sighed. "I told you last night just how much I love your tight, little backside, but in case there's any question, then yeah, I most definitely like what I see. A whole helluva lot."

She laughed again, her tone low and throaty. "I want you inside me, Nick. Let's make our audience happy."

He bit back a curse as guilt washed through him. He wanted to do as she asked. His cock felt ready to split out of his skin if he didn't, but goddamn he wouldn't hurt her. "Are you sure about this, Stephie? It's not too late to change your mind."

She glanced over her shoulder, devotion burned hot in the depths of her gaze. "I trust you, honey. I know you'll listen if I ask you to stop."

He nodded, his heart beating faster with the honesty in her eyes, her words. She'd called him honey again, and he wanted to be. He wanted to be her honey for as long as she would let him. "All right, but one single second of pain, and I—"

"Nick, shut up and make me feel good." She reached behind her and took his hand, brought it between her thighs and rubbed their joined fingers over her slick vulva. "I've gotten us started, now don't make me do all the work."

He chuckled. "*You* are amazing."

"Shh… Less talk, more action."

Stephie moved her fingers with his, petting herself, whimpering her pleasure. Nick lathered his pulsating shaft with the moisture from her body. Holding his breath, he guided himself to the edge of her buttocks, then slowly eased in. She moaned as his straining head penetrated her, then he pushed deeper and she froze. He froze as well and swore.

"I'm hurting you, aren't I?"

She nodded. "Oh, Nick, I'm so sorry. I wanted this to work. I wanted to make your fantasy come true, but I'm too small."

He heard the disappointment in her words, the self-accusation that followed them, and pulled her back against his chest. No way would he allow her to be upset over something as asinine as fulfilling his fantasy. "It's okay, sweetheart," he breathed near her ear, "it was a stupid idea. I should never have said anything."

"But I wanted to..." She trailed off then wriggled in his arms. He moved back and released her. She shot to her feet and smiled. "I have an idea. I'll be right back."

Without another word, she darted away, her taut rear end tormenting him even as she disappeared through the sliding glass doors. Less than a minute had passed when she returned, filling his doorway with all her womanly assets exposed for his viewing.

Nick gave her body a long leisurely look then met her sparkling eyes. "What did you get?"

She tossed him a small black tube of Analube then dropped to her position in front of him, leaning against the lounge chair. "I'm not too small. We just need more moisture."

He frowned at the excitement in her tone, the tube of lubrication in his hand. "This isn't worth it, Stephie. I told you, it isn't a big deal."

"It is to me," she said firmly. "Now let's do this the right way."

Nick expelled a long sigh. What was the point of living out a fantasy if he was too tense to enjoy it? Still, it mattered to her and so he had to try. He squeezed a generous supply of Analube onto his palm and covered his fingers with the gel. Holding his breath, he brought his fingers to her crack and parted her tight cheeks. He slid two fingers in and fondled her with the tips. She reared back against him and moaned.

"Do you like that?" he asked, almost afraid of her answer.

Her words came out on a pant. "Oh, yes. Yes, I like it."

He let free his breath, but still moved cautiously. She'd taken two fingers last night without a problem, but that didn't mean she could take the rest of him. "How about another finger."

"Please," she purred.

His tension settling with her throaty tone, he added another finger and thrust them together against the slippery walls of her buttocks.

"Oh, God, Nick," she wailed. "That's amazing. Absolutely amazing."

His balls drew beyond tight and he gritted his teeth. If she were lying he would kill her. But no, she wouldn't lie about something like this. Not after how open she'd been with him last night. "Do you want more?"

"No," she growled. "I want you. I want to feel your cock in me."

Trembling, he removed his fingers and eased the first inch of his erection into her ass. She writhed against him, and her hands fell to the chair's seat in fists. "Oh, yes! More, Nick. I want more."

He pushed in farther, biting down on his lip as her anus contracted around him, the friction so tense it brought tears to his eyes. Biting down harder, until he tasted blood, he eased the rest of the way in, and closed his eyes at the immense pressure. "Am I hurting you, sweetheart? Do you want me to stop."

"No. No," she panted. "Don't stop. Ride me, Nick."

"I don't know if I can." He was every damned bit as hard as he'd been last night, maybe more so. One move was all it would take and he would be coming in her pretty little behind. Reaching around, he filled his hands with her supple breasts, then inched back slowly and rocked.

"Oh, yeah. Yes." Stephie's knuckles shone white as ivory against the chair, her chest heaving and sweaty beneath his palms, her heart knocking madly against his own through her back. "Oh, God, Nick. I'm going to explode."

He buried his face in her hair, inhaling her fragrance, and rode faster, took her deeper, then nearly screamed when the orgasm burst through him, blinding him to everything but the woman in his arms and the depths of emotion in his heart.

Long moments passed before he could breathe normally, and even then he was too weak to do anything more than cling to her, kiss her golden head, and praise the heavens above for bringing him to her. He'd known he'd felt something for her nearly from the moment they'd met. Those feelings had grown considerably when she revealed her darkest secrets to him last night. Now he knew just how much he cared.

He loved her. Not because she fulfilled his fantasy, but because after all she'd been through, she trusted him enough to allow it to happen, because she was genuine, and had a laugh that could light the darkest of days. Beyond that she was just plain incredible. So good, so giving, so…so amazingly rigid in his arms.

Worry replaced the warmth in his heart, and he eased out and turned her until she faced him. She stared at him openmouthed. "Did you just say you love me, Nick?"

Chapter 11

Stephanie bit the inside of her cheek, holding her breath, waiting for a response. Dear God, was it possible he could love her? She knew she cared about him, was all but positive he was her Mr. Right, but that he could feel the same way for her, or something even stronger, well...it was just too unbelievable to be true.

Nick remained silent, expressionless. He slid his arms from around her, and the hope that welled in her heart crashed to her feet like a lead a balloon. He was *not* retreating. He couldn't be, not after what he'd said. Unless the words had been a mistake, the kind of thing that was accidentally voiced in the heat of passion. That sort of thing did happen, or so her friends had often told her. But no, he wouldn't make that huge of a mistake. He was smarter than that! Wasn't he?

"Did you say love me?" she repeated in a whisper.

He straightened and tugged on his shorts, retrieved his shirt, then finally looked back at her. Regret weighed heavily in his gaze, and churned her stomach with acid.

"I don't know, did I?"

Stephanie's breath drew in on a painful gasp. *Did he?*

Why, of all the idiotic, degrading, downright horrible things to ask. He was just as big of a dickhead as Greg. No, Nick was far worse with the way he'd kissed her, touched her and gotten under her skin until there was no getting him back out.

She'd wondered if he'd felt the same way, sensed the gentle stirrings of attachment. It was beyond clear that he most certainly did not. She'd be damned if she let him think his little misspeak had upset her. Bad girl Stephie might not be around to toss out some smart-ass remark, but Stephanie could certainly come up with something on her own. She was a grown woman, fully capable of dealing with the hurt that pressed at her heart, the emotion that burned at the back of her eyes. She just had to ignore it, force it back and act like she didn't give a shit. It shouldn't be that hard to do, she just had to mimic Nick's actions.

Squaring her shoulders, she came to her feet and pulled on her shorts. She gathered the rest of her clothes, pasted on a smile and looked up at him. "It sounded like that's what you said, but I'm sure it was just an accident, a heat of the moment kind of thing. I know I've made the same mistake a number of times."

He flinched, sorrow flitting through his gaze, and for an instant she regretted her words, then she remembered how coldly he pulled away from her, how nonchalantly he asked her to clarify what he'd said. For that he deserved her callousness. Hell, he deserved to be tied to the anchor and drowned.

Stephanie smiled harder, shrugged as if they were talking about something as insignificant as the weather, while inside she felt ready to implode. "You've done it before too, right, accidentally told someone you loved them? I think it's a natural reaction to say those words right after you've had a really good fuck."

Swallowing visibly, Nick crossed his arms and nodded. "Sure. Lots of times."

But it didn't look like he had. He looked miserable, his sea green eyes dark and stormy, his forehead knit, and misery etched into every line on his face.

Damn it, why did he have to look that way? It would be so much easier to pretend like she didn't care, if he'd stop acting like someone stepped on his puppy and broke its scrawny little neck.

"That's what I thought," she said flippantly. "Just a natural reaction."

Aware how close she was to breaking down, Stephanie started for the glass door that led to his bedroom. She veered past his bed, struggling for something to say, conversation that wouldn't open the dam of tears holed up at the back of her throat. "I guess we should find something for lunch, huh?"

"Yeah." Nick's footsteps padded quietly behind her as she made her way into the joint kitchen and dining area. The sound stopped, and she fought the urge to turn around and see what he was doing, see if his expression had changed any. Or even better, his mind. Maybe he'd merely been confused by her question. Yeah right. 'Did you say you love me?' was about as cut and dried as a girl could get.

"Why don't you get cleaned up, and I'll throw something together?" he asked.

Nodding her response, she went to the cabin door and tugged it open.

"Stephanie?"

Her heart turned over at the sound of her name on his tongue, her real name. She looked back against her better judgment, against the emotional ache that tensed every bone in her body, and met his eyes. "Yes, Nick?"

He stared at her from the center of the room, his hands buried in the pockets of his shorts and a frown pulling at his lips. The tic flitted to life in his jaw, but she knew better than to think it was passion this time around. "Do you wanna eat in your cabin? You don't have to…it's just that I have a lot of work to get done, and I thought…"

And he thought that way he wouldn't have to face her with the realization of what an ass he was being? Yeah, that made perfect sense. She forced yet another smile. "It's okay, Nick. My cabin's fine. Send it down when it's ready."

Stephanie didn't wait around to hear his answer. She knew it would be something along the lines of 'Thank God'. Of course, he wouldn't say those precise words, but that would be the gist of it. And he'd be right. It was a thankful thing he'd inadvertently pointed out where the lines of their relationship were drawn.

They were lovers. Weekend lovers. And he wasn't Mr. Right, but merely Mr. Close Enough. The cure to her seven-year itch. Greg's last minute replacement. Nothing more or less. He accepted the truth, it was high time she did too.

* * * * *

Just when things looked like they couldn't get any worse, he had to go and check his goddamned e-mail. Nick scowled at the message on his laptop screen. He knew he couldn't prolong his decision about the world news spread forever, but he'd hoped to wait another week or two.

There wouldn't be a couple more weeks, or even a couple more days. His secretary had sent him this e-mail shortly after noon on Friday, stating Anderson was tired of waiting for Nick's decision, he needed a firm 'yes' or 'no' by Monday morning. She also said she'd been trying to get a hold of him by cell phone since then.

It was no wonder she hadn't been able to get through. He hadn't done anything business related since the moment he'd stepped foot on the *Hidden Desire,* including turning on his mobile phone. All right, he'd worked on his local news column minimally this morning and again this afternoon, but not enough to count. Sure as hell not enough to earn a paycheck.

The urgent response flag flashed to life on the computer's monitor, drawing Nick's mind back to the situation at hand. He had to make a choice, and he had to make it soon. And really when he stopped and thought about it, it wasn't even all that difficult.

He didn't have anyone keeping him in the area, someone he cared about who returned those feelings. Maybe his little sister fell into that grouping, but he knew better than to think Emily wouldn't be excited to have him out of her life for weeks at a time. She could do whatever she wanted, run naked through the city streets and not have to worry about him finding out. Everyone would be ecstatic, everyone but him.

Shit, that wasn't true either. He'd wanted to take the job since the moment it was offered to him. He'd just needed an impetus to propel him into action. The little blond honey downstairs had given him that push and so much more.

He scrubbed a hand over his face as Stephie's unwanted image entered his mind. How the hell could he ever have believed she cared about him? She looked horrified, stricken to think he might love her. And the way she defaced his unplanned admission as a natural reaction to really good sex? No, not really good sex—really good fucking.

Damn it, how could've he been so wrong about her?

The way she'd opened up to him about her past, the way she acted toward him—calling him honey and kissing him with such blind emotion— she made him believe that she cared, made him think that she loved him too. For a moment as they stood on the deck, he'd held out hope he'd misread her reaction, that she wasn't horrified, but in shock. Then she'd turned away and changed the subject, coldly refuted him when all he was trying to do was gauge her response to his blurted confession.

Good girl or not, she obviously had come on this boat for sex and nothing more. Well, he was a big boy. He could handle being the meaningless weekend fling. The stand-in for another man, one she'd grown tired of and left behind the same way she'd do to him come tomorrow afternoon. Yeah, he could handle that. How difficult could it be? All he had to do was follow Stephie's lead.

Pushing thoughts of her from his mind, Nick turned back to the computer screen, and sealed his fate with a simple yes.

* * * * *

Stephanie refused to eat dinner alone in her cabin. It was a gorgeous night, her last on the *Hidden Desire* before she returned to the boredom of weekday life. A boredom, she realized now, that wasn't such a bad thing. She might be a stiff-suit financial analyst, hesitant to let her guard down during working hours, but at least at Gamble & Net she was respected, used for more than someone's convenient plaything.

Oh, hell, that wasn't fair, just like her cruel assessment of Nick's earlier actions hadn't been. She was the one who'd approached him, strutting about in her itty-bitty bikini, sticking her fingers in her crotch and masturbating for the sheer pleasure of taunting him into her arms. She'd more or less told him she wasn't interested in anything beyond sex. It wasn't his fault if with his unspoken agreement came the stinging sensation that someone had stuck a knife in her heart and twisted.

There was only one way to put things right between them, and that was to bring them back to the level they'd been on when they first met—strangers with a mutual desire to get down and dirty. He'd already put distance between them by asking her to take lunch in her cabin, all she had to do was play her part, and approach him with the same 'been around the block, bad girl attitude' she'd had in the beginning.

How hard could that be?

Really, really hard. The answer came to Stephanie, correction, Stephie, twenty minutes later when she found Nick in his bedroom, typing away on his laptop, his hair pushed in all directions as if he'd continually run his fingers through it. He was so deep in thought he didn't even look up as she stood in his doorway and stared at him.

He looked so defenseless right now. So much like the last man on the earth who would intentionally set out to hurt her. But no, she knew that hadn't been the case. Once she'd had a chance to cool down, she'd realized he really had told her he loved her on accident. The regret in his eyes should have made that clear from the start.

He wasn't a dickhead, nowhere near to the two-timing sleaze-ball she'd first compared him to. He was merely human. He'd misspoken, claimed something that wasn't true, that she had absolutely no right to even believe in, considering how little time they'd known each other. She couldn't hold a mistake against him forever, not when she could be doing what she came on this boat for in the first place, and taking full advantage of their last night together.

"So, did you have a chance to get your work done yet, captain?" Stephie asked in a husky voice, sashaying into his bedroom like she had every right to be there.

Nick jerked his head up and stared at her in open surprise. He lowered his gaze, taking in her body in the tight black dress, just the way she'd hoped he would. He stalled on the triangle cut over her breasts to reveal a generous helping of cleavage, and the tic worked in his jaw. Heat rushed through her body, dampening her g-string in a way only he could make happen with such a simple look.

He stood and met her eyes. "Actually, I was just finishing up."

He punched something on the laptop's keyboard, then closed its cover and stuck it back in the cubbyhole over his bed. Burying his hands in the pockets of his shorts, he turned back to her. His expression was no longer that of shock, but weighed down by a myriad of emotions. He opened his mouth as if to say something, then stopped.

Clearing his throat, he tried again. "About earlier —"

"You don't have to explain, Nick." Stephie quickly cut him off, not about to delve back in to a moment she'd already put behind her. "We're both adults. Old enough to acknowledge what's happening between us is just sex. Don't get me wrong, I think you're a great person, but I'm not in the market for a relationship." Maybe she would never again be ready for a real relationship, considering how sick she'd felt over the end of something they'd never even shared in the first place.

She pushed that thought aside, and flashed her best bad girl grin. "Anyway, I noticed what a nice night it was and thought maybe you'd want to have dinner with me out on your deck. And then maybe after we can share some..." She flicked her tongue out, slowly rimming the edges of her brightly painted lips, then pulled it back in with a soft slurping sound. "...dessert."

Swallowing loud enough to hear halfway across the room, Nick averted his gaze and strolled past her to the opened windows. A gentle wind rolled in, bringing with it the fresh scent of the lake. "It is nice out," he commented with his back to her, his posture too stiff to be comfortable. "Finally a breeze."

Baffled by his rigid stance in light of how openly she'd agreed to his unspoken request they be lovers and nothing more, Stephie went to him. She laid her hand on the corded muscle of his arm, and he jerked under her touch, spinning back to stare at her.

"Dinner's good," he bit out.

She frowned at his continued edginess. Why on earth was he acting so base? He wanted her for sex. She was making it more than clear she wanted the same. He ought to be dancing on air, not walking on pins and needles. He must not have expected her to come back to his room tonight. Well, if that was the case and he merely needed time to readjust his thinking, she would be more than happy to indulge him.

She rose on tiptoe, skimming the softness of her breasts along the hard planes of his body, and brushed a kiss over his mouth. Before he could respond, she drew back and crossed to the sliding glass door. She pulled it open, then turned back and winked. "I'll be waiting for you on the deck, Nick. Just let me know if you need help with anything. Anything at all. Just call my name."

* * * * *

Nick blew out a long breath as Stephie disappeared through the sliding glass door onto his deck. What the hell game was she playing now? He would've guessed the role of the bad girl, but she hadn't tasted bad when she kissed him. She'd tasted good. Very good. Like a woman he could spend his life drinking in, one kiss at a time. Only that wasn't why she'd come back to his room cloaked in a skintight dress that started at the rise of her succulent breasts and ended way too close to her junction.

No, she wasn't here to kiss, to exchange words of love or anything even close to them. She was here to have sex, and it was his job to see that it happened.

Resigned to his fate, Nick threw together the quickest meal he could come up with. He selected a bottle of red wine to compliment the dinner and, grabbing two wineglasses, made his way onto the deck. Stephie sat facing the water, her back to him and her golden hair shimmering in the light of the rising moon.

"I hope you like Capellini Pomodoro."

She turned and smiled, flashed her teeth. "If you think I won't, we could always skip right to dessert. I'll even let you choose which end we start on. Though I have to say, I quite enjoyed the ass end."

Nick's balls drew tight with the memory of thrusting his cock into her supple backside. He'd enjoyed it too, but only as much as he enjoyed every other inch of her body, and all the other things that made her the extraordinary woman she was.

Setting down the wine bottle and glasses, he stuffed his hands into his pockets. They were safe there, secured from the temptation to pull her into his arms and ravish her mouth with needy kisses. "As appealing as that sounds, we need nourishment. I haven't fed you nearly enough this weekend."

She laughed throatily and, stroking the lip of the wineglass he'd placed before her, sent her gaze over the length of him. She returned to his eyes and growled low in her throat. "Trust me, Nick, you're all the nourishment I need."

A groan escaped his lips before he could stop it, and she laughed again, this time the sound far more authentic. "Are you sure about eating first, because it sounds to me like there's an animal inside you just waiting to get out and be satisfied."

"We need food," he said resolutely.

Doing his best to fortify his resolve they did indeed need to eat, Nick retrieved their dinner, then sat down in the chair next to Stephie's. Scratch that, a chair that was on top of Stephie's. They were so close together they might as well have started out in each other's laps and called it good.

As if she sensed the direction of his thoughts and couldn't agree more, she reached over and rested her hand on his thigh. It remained there for all of two seconds, before she moved it lower, skimming her fingers along his shaft through the thin material of his shorts. He moaned when he grew hard beneath her touch.

Sonofabitch. She didn't play fair. She had on a tiny excuse for a dress, her creamy breasts all but sticking through the center and God only knew what beneath, and she was fondling him. How the hell was he supposed to eat?

"Comfy, huh?" she purred.

"Yeah, very quaint." He reached for his fork, determined to see this meal through. Stephie's lusty words halted him before he could make contact with the utensil.

"Petting your cock makes me very wet, Nick. I feel like I could come just from touching you. What do you say I go beneath your shorts?"

"Stephie," he warned, even as she slid her hand beneath his waistband and twined her fingers around him.

Stroking his throbbing erection, she pushed her chair back and slid to her knees. With her free hand, she caressed the exposed flesh of his leg, then dipped beneath the edge of his shorts to tease over his inner thigh.

She moved higher still, and flashed a smile that said she would win this battle. "I wore a g-string for you, Nick. I thought you could pull it up against my crack. Or maybe bury the front against my pussy. I bet that would feel good too."

"Stephie," he warned again, a groan punctuating the word as she took his testicles into her hand, cradling and shaping them, kindling a fire of endless need that was quickly demolishing any hope Nick had of making it through dinner.

"This weekend's almost over and, other than my hairbrush we haven't used any of the toys in my cabin. I saw lots of good stuff. But maybe we don't need to use any of those things. Maybe your hands are all I need."

She stopped her sweet torture and drew both her hands away. For a second, he breathed a sigh of relief. Then she spread his legs apart and wedged her body between his thighs, wriggled against his rock hard member, and he knew all hope was lost.

"Will you spank me, Nick?" she breathed, sliding her palms along his chest and up around his neck. She licked her pouty red lips — so near to his own — gazed up at him through eyes rich with passion. "Will you spank me and tell me what a naughty girl I've been? I'd like to feel your hand on my bottom. You know what else I'd like? I'd like to feel your big, thick cock buried deep inside me, making me scream with ecstasy. I'd like that to happen right now."

Fingering his neck with the tips of her nails, Stephie ran her tongue over the seam of his mouth. Nick parted his lips, knowing he was already too far gone to go back even if that's what he wanted. It wasn't what he wanted. Not when she was rubbing her curvy, little body against him, grinding his throbbing erection between her thighs with mindless urgency. An urgency that made him forget about everything but curling his arms around her and granting her every wish.

She swiped at his mouth again, edging her tongue past his lips. He darted out his own, needing to taste her, to forage on her sweetness, the goodness he knew rested in her heart. Just when he would have made contact, Stephie drew back.

"So, what do you say?" she asked in a smoky tone. "Do we eat dinner, or risk sampling dessert first?"

He chuckled. The answer to that question was prodding against her thighs. He responded aloud to appease her. "Who needs dinner, when dessert tastes this good."

Her musical laughter lit up the night, warming his heart as he pulled her tighter against him and stabbed his tongue past her lips. She suckled back with raw need, stealing his breath and whatever logic hadn't already left him.

She moved back after several long seconds, gasping for air. "I knew you'd see things my way. Like I told you yesterday, you and I are meant to be together."

Nick's ears pricked at her words. Hope burst forth, and he met her eyes, asking questions with his own. Was all that dirty talk just a show? Had she realized just how right they were together? How much he truly did care?

Cupping her cheek in his hand, he asked, "What do you mean, sweetheart?"

She shot him a triumphant grin. "Just like I said, captain, we were meant to be together. You and I were born to fuck."

* * * * *

She'd called him honey. She'd called him a lot of other things that weren't nearly so nice as he tore her little black dress off and ground himself into her tight body, but all Nick could think about was that one word. She'd said it again when he'd carried her to his bed and made love to her the leisurely way he'd been dying to do all day. And a third time as she drifted off to sleep, her head on his chest, her hair in a chaotic blond tumble, and her long, slender fingers splayed over his heart.

Had she realized she'd said the word any of those times? The first two times she'd been on the verge of coming. But not the last. The last time she'd been stretched out over his chest, her breathing growing shallow as sleep slowly claimed her. To utter such an intimacy in a moment like that, at least a part of her had to care about him. It was that same part, the same genuine version of her he held sleeping in his arms now.

Nick brushed her hair away from her face and smiled down at her lips curved up in a pout. She looked completely innocent, completely faultless, and completely like what he needed most in his life. But of course none of that was real. Merely a facade brought about by the shadows of night and his desire to make it real.

It was a damned good thing he'd agreed to take the world news position before she showed up in his bedroom. If she had showed up first and allowed him to make love to her, kiss her with all the emotions that burned within him, he'd have likely done something really stupid. Something like, convincing her to open her eyes and heart and see that he really did care about her. That he'd do anything to make her see how legitimate his love was, even pass over a position that would take him out of the area and away from the comfort of her arms for weeks at a time.

Yeah. It was a damned good thing he'd taken that job offer when he did, because none of this was real and tomorrow Stephie would be gone.

Chapter 12

Stephie was gone, and a hell of a lot sooner than Nick had expected.

It shouldn't have surprised him to wake to an empty bed, the tattered remains of a lacy black g-string the only sign she'd been in his room at all, but it did. He'd planned to wake up first. To have time to hold her and hang onto his fantasy that there was something real between them awhile longer. Instead, he'd slept in 'til goddamned ten o'clock.

He sneered at the bright red numbers of the digital clock next to his bed. He should have set the alarm for dawn. It would've woken Stephie up as well, but he could have rolled over and pinned her in place, used his added weight to stop her from running back to her own deck. And then when they docked later this afternoon he could have turned himself over to the cops for manhandling a woman who had already been through too damned much in her life.

Hell, it wasn't Stephie's fault he felt like someone had ripped his heart out, one muscle strand at a time. From the start, she'd more or less made it clear all she wanted from him was sex. He was the one who'd tried to turn this thing between them into more, who'd gotten his hopes up a little higher each time she called him 'honey'. Even last night as he'd told himself time and again nothing between them was real, that today they'd part ways forever and be better off for it, he'd still hoped, still prayed she'd change her mind.

She hadn't changed her mind. She'd left his bed the moment she realized she was in it, most likely with disgust etched out on her face. And if that wasn't concrete proof the only thing they had together was chemistry, then nothing was.

Nick swung his legs to the side of the bed and, squinting against the sunlight, looked through the sliding glass door to the lake. A light chop stirred the water, enough to tell him last night's breeze hadn't faded, and the boisterous cry of gulls swept in through the opened windows.

Just another day in paradise. Too bad paradise was about to end.

Their hours left on the *Hidden Desire* were quickly fading. His time left serving as the pleasure cruiser's captain nearly as short. He might as well use the remainder of their time together to its fullest extent, and give Stephie what she wanted. The *only* thing she wanted from him. An easy lay.

* * * * *

It was all Stephanie could do to keep from beating her head against the bathroom wall as she packed the minimal makeup and hair supplies she'd brought along. Jesus, how stupid could she be? She'd called Nick honey. Not once, but three times!

The first two he might not have heard, they'd both been way too involved in the moment for much in the way of thought, but the last time they'd been lying together on his bed, neither saying a thing. The moment the word slipped from her mouth, he'd stiffened, and she knew beyond a doubt he'd heard her loud and clear.

To add salt to the wound, she'd fallen asleep in his arms.

Okay, so that part had been on purpose. The way he'd held her last night, made love to her so slow and sweet, as if he couldn't get enough, it had seemed perfect. Like he really did love her. Like he wanted something more from her than sex.

Of course, he didn't feel that way, but for a little while she'd been able to pretend. To hold him in her arms and listen to his peaceful breathing as he slept, treasure the quiet beat of his heart beneath her ear one last time before they said goodbye. And they would say goodbye, very soon and forever.

Hot and very unwelcome tears dashed to the front of her eyes. Stephanie wiped them away and squared her shoulders. Today it was more important than ever that Stephie be in control. Stephie had a hardened heart and a bad girl attitude. She didn't cry over meaningless relationships that ended before they'd even begun. No, she traipsed into a room like she owned the place and left that room with any man she wanted on her arm.

Yes, bold as brass Stephie was needed here. Immediately.

After all, they still had another four hours before they headed back to shore. While Nick might not want her in the long run, it would be foolish not to take advantage of his presence in the short-run. She'd go to him and give him all he wanted. The *only* thing he wanted from her. An easy fuck.

* * * * *

Nick finished slicing the antipasto he'd prepared for lunch, and placed the platter on the tray next to a loaf of fresh baked bread. He grabbed a bottle of white wine and two glasses, set them on the tray as well then headed for Stephie's deck. He'd made it to the rear of the boat when she appeared at the top of the stairwell to her cabin. She smiled at him, her cheeks blushing with vivid color, as if she'd been caught in the midst of doing something naughty. Knowing her, she probably had been.

"Nick," she said softly.

He nodded to the tray in his hands. "I was just bringing your lunch down."

She glanced at the wine bottle and glasses, and her smile turned to the eat-'em-alive one he knew he'd never be able to forget. "I guess great minds really do think alike. I was on my way up to see if you needed help with anything."

Catching the way she raised her eyebrows when she voiced the word 'anything', he shifted his gaze away. It landed smack in the center of her chest. Another too tight top, this one pink with little white flowers, pushed her generous breasts all but over the edge. She wore her cross necklace again, and an itty-bitty pair of white canvas shorts.

Damn, didn't the woman own anything that covered more than her navel?

She laid her hand on his arm, and he jerked his attention back to her smiling face. "So, where do you want to eat, Nick?"

The real question was 'what did he want to eat', and the answer wasn't the food on the tray in his hands, but the woman who stood before him. "It's up to you."

Stephie licked her lips and peered up at him from under thick lashes, heat smoldered her eyes to dark chocolate. He could read her thoughts as easily as if she'd voiced them. She wanted the same thing for lunch that he did. Maybe it was a good thing she'd soon be out of his life. If she stayed in it much longer he was liable to starve to death.

"We probably should eat, huh?" she asked.

"It would be a good idea."

She stuck her lower lip out in a pout, and nodded. "Okay."

Nick chuckled at the somberness of her tone. "Do you really have to make it sound like it'll kill you? I used to take pride in my culinary skills."

"You're a great cook, Nick. It's just that you're great at a lot of other things too. I have food at home, what I don't have is you." Her voice wavered, and though he knew it was inconceivable, she looked like she was going to cry.

Her fiery red lips tipped back up in a saucy grin, and she gave his forearm a playful squeeze. "So, what do you say, captain? Do we eat, or do we play a game?"

Yep, it was inconceivable that she'd ever cry over him. For that matter, ever cry in front of him at all. He might as well focus on this game. "What exactly did you have in mind?"

"Stephie's House of Flavors."

He laughed loudly. "Is that the game where we cover each other in flavored body oils, then see who can lick it off the fastest?"

"Something like that. Expect you forgot the part where if you don't guess what the flavor is, you have to keep licking until you get it right."

Licking her supple body until he guessed right. Now that sounded like a whole hell of a lot of fun. And what if he never guessed right? Did that mean he got to keep her in his bed indefinitely? "Ah, fuck it, why the hell not."

Stephie let free a vigorous laugh, the sound carrying on the wind and spiraling endless warmth deep inside him. She met his eyes, her own filled with humor and what looked remarkably like adoration. "Oh, honey, the way you give in to all my fantasies, it's no wonder I fell in love with you so fast."

The air rushed from Nick's lungs and the tray clattered noisily to his feet, white wine breaking free of its glass confines and soaking everything in its path. He dropped to his knees in a delayed attempt to stop the food from hitting the deck as well, then cursed when antipasto strewed in a haphazard pile of lettuce, meats and cheeses.

He scowled at the food another second, then forgot all about it as her words repeated in his head, restoring hope he'd given up on and all but bursting the walls of his heart. He shot to his feet and opened his mouth to ask her to repeat her words. Stephie started coughing, scratch that, gagging in a mad fit and halted his efforts. She pounded at her chest, gasping for air then all at once her coughs turned to laughter—fake laughter. He knew the sound of her real laugh, and this wasn't it.

She lifted her slender shoulders in a shrug and shot him a grin that showed her teeth. "You know what they say about pesky little natural reactions. Sometimes the words come out even before you have the really good fuck."

* * * * *

Stephanie tried to hold back her grimace as Nick coasted the *Hidden Desire* into her slip at Murphy's Harbor. Unfortunately, it didn't work any better than holding back the tears that welled in her throat.

What a horrible ending to an incredible weekend. Sure it'd had its ups and downs, but all in all it had been perfect. Perfect in a way she'd never have experienced if it hadn't been for catching Greg with his penis in another woman's mouth. She supposed she owed him something for that. Maybe she'd return the blender he'd brought to her house for daiquiris a few weeks before—right after she broke it in half and snipped off its cord.

The warmth of the sun left her back and the deck in front of her fell into shadows. She inhaled the air, the scent of man clinging to her senses. Her man. Her Nick. At least he had been for a little while.

She turned and took in his solid form, the muscles in his arms and legs and the dark stubble that lined his strong jaw, and heaved a sigh over the loss of a man she'd never even had in the first place. Maybe she could see him again. It was feasible he would agree to another pleasure cruise, just so long as emotions weren't involved. At least emotions he wasn't aware existed.

She forced a saucy smile to her lips and stepped closer, tipped her head back. "So, is the boat already reserved for next weekend, captain?"

Nick shrugged. "As far as I know."

Stephanie tensed with the indifference of his tone, the firm set of his mouth. Even his eyes looked off limits, their typical sea green shade as dark and hard as flint. Had he already pushed her from his mind? No, that wasn't possible, not so quickly. She hadn't expected him to get teary-eyed over her departure, but still he was a compassionate man, a man who'd shown her wonderful things these last few days, a man whose fantasies she'd fulfilled. At the very least, he could give her a smile.

"Maybe we could arrange something for the weekend after that," she said, all but begging him with her eyes to say yes.

The edges of his mouth tipped up, easing the tautness of her limbs. He nodded toward shore. "You'll have to talk to Don at the check-in desk. I'm not sure who's going to be running the *Hidden Desire* after this weekend."

She gasped, anxiety surmounting anew. *"What?"*

"This was my last trip out."

His what? This could *not* be happening. He couldn't be leaving his role of captain behind. How would she ever see him again! "Don't you enjoy your job?"

Nick scrubbed his hand over his face, then up through his sin-black hair, further upsetting the windblown waves. "This isn't my job. At least not my full-time one."

It wasn't? Oh God, they really didn't know anything about each other. She didn't even know what he did for a living. "What do you do?" she blurted.

The tic flitted to life in his jaw, as if he were leery of telling her, but he answered all the same. "I'm a newspaper columnist for *The Tribune*. Well, I was anyway. I accepted a position with *The Opportunist*. I'm gonna be traveling a lot, so I won't be able to keep working here on the weekends."

"Oh. That makes sense." And royally sucked ass.

Was it possible he was making it up? Telling her he had a new job, one that took him away from home, so he wouldn't have to see her again? It didn't sound like the

Nick she knew, but hell, she didn't really know him at all. At least, nothing beyond his fantasies and the size of his masculinity.

Her heart hurt with the realization of how little they truly did know about one another. How could she ever have believed herself in love with him, a complete stranger? At least, close enough to one. She forced a fresh smile to her lips. "I should go. My dog...I have a beagle...she's probably lonely."

"I bet she is, probably been crying for you since you left."

Yep, and tonight she'd have company. Stephanie tamped back the thought. She wasn't going to cry over him. Okay, so she might, but she wasn't going to plan it into her evening routine as a positive. "Probably," she agreed softly.

Nick's smile drew a little higher. "I guess this is goodbye."

"Yeah." Goodbye. Good riddance. Don't call me, I'll call you.

Son of a bitch, why did they have to meet? It would have been so easy for her to pick another man to take with her on the *Hidden Desire*. But no, she'd had to go for the captain. The Adonis that caught her eye the moment she'd stepped from her car.

What a dumbass.

She waited a second, waited to see if he'd kiss her one last time, or at least shake her hand, but he remained immobile. A sob made its way up her throat, lodging there so tightly she could barely breathe. Before her tears could follow suit, she bent and scooped up her duffel bag, hefted its thick strap over her shoulder, and with a final mock salute, she made her way over the side of the boat and onto the dock.

She'd almost reached the shore, when Nick called her name. She quickened her pace, refusing to turn around, to have to look upon his handsome face and say yet another painful goodbye. He called her name a second time, louder, and she knew she didn't have a choice.

Drawing a steadying breath, she turned back. "What?"

He stood halfway down the dock, looking almost as if he'd started to come after her—too bad she knew otherwise. "I just...I had a really good time."

She bit back the sob that threatened to break free, and nodded. "Yeah. Me too."

He flashed a smile, a real one that brought warmth to his eyes. "See you around?"

"You bet." In her dreams for the rest of her life, Stephanie knew as she hurried for her Beemer and the safety of a world far away from Nick Calanetti.

Chapter 13

"You really had it bad for Greg, huh?"

Stephanie shook her head free of its haze at the sound of her secretary's voice. She swiveled from staring out the second floor window of Gamble & Net, and met Amelia's gaze. The way her dark eyebrows were drawn together and her forehead knit, she looked like she expected an answer. Too bad for her, Stephanie had only caught the tail end of the question.

"Greg?" she prompted, reaching across her desk to take the offered mail bundle.

Amelia's brow furrowed further and she fisted a hand at her snugly clothed hip. "Chisolm. The guy you were dating 'til two weeks ago when you found out what an asshole he is. Remember, that Greg?"

"Oh. That Greg." The two-timing jerk she'd buried in the farthest recesses of her mind, along with several other things she'd just as soon forget. Stephanie sighed over those other 'left to be nameless' things, then quickly flushed them from her thoughts. "Trust me, the only thing I had bad where that man's concerned, was judgment."

Amelia laughed shortly then sobered. "Well, if it isn't Greg, what gives, girl? You sure look miserable about something."

"I need a vacation," Stephanie said, sinking back into her chair. Somewhere that palm trees grew in abundance and Mr. Right loomed around every corner. And maybe on her fast track to Fantasy Land she could stop and pluck a few thousand dollars from the money tree orchard.

"Then maybe you ought to think about taking one. I know just how much time you have saved up. You're way overdue for some fun in the sun." With a last meaningful look, Amelia went to the door. She turned back when she reached it, and smiled. "Whatever's got you so down, cheer up. The weekend starts in less than four hours, and it's supposed to be a great one."

Right, the weekend, Stephanie thought wryly as her friend pulled the door closed behind her. Those long, lonely two days and three nights where she sat on her couch, watching movies with her dog and pouting.

Amelia was right. She was miserable. A miserable excuse for a human being. She had to get past this melancholy, this endless state of lethargy that had claimed her since that fateful weekend aboard that boat with that guy she wasn't about to name.

What she needed was a date with a complete stranger. Someone she could get to know slowly, over many, many days, and then if and when the time came she was ready, they could take that next step and consider a physical relationship.

Yes, she needed a date with a stranger, and what better place to look than the personal ads. Who knew, maybe Mr. Right was just a phone call away.

Kicking off her dark suede pumps, Stephanie reclined back in her chair and spread the paper out on her lap. She turned the pages slowly, searching for the personal section, waiting for a name to pop out at her. When one finally did, along with a very sexy headshot, she screamed. Loudly. Very loudly.

The door to her office burst open and Amelia rushed in, her normally dark complexion stark white. "What's the matter? Did something happen? Are you okay?"

No, she wasn't okay. The guy she wasn't supposed to think about was in her paper. What the hell was he doing in...oh...right...he was a newspaper columnist. How could she have forgotten? Maybe because they'd only discussed that fact for a total of two seconds—the rest of their trip had been spent on much more meaningful pursuits.

Feeling heat rise into her cheeks at the memory of all those things she'd done with Nick, things she'd only dreamt of doing before she met him, Stephanie averted her gaze. "I'm fine. I didn't mean to scare you. There's just a...a sale this weekend at Shoe World, and I really need a new pair of sandals."

Yep, that excuse ranked right up there with sucks real bad. At least it wasn't a lie. She did need new sandals. Hers smelled like wine and antipasto, and reminded her of one of the most idiotic moments of her life. That instant when she'd blurted her love to Nick, then coolly played it out as a natural reaction to sex. Except those hadn't been her exact words. She'd actually said fucking.

Thank God, she'd left her potty mouth back on the boat. She could just imagine her coworker's faces if she started talking that way around the office.

"You sure you're all right, girl?" Amelia asked, pulling her back to the here and now. "You're not acting like yourself."

And how was that? Boring? Quiet? Like she had nothing better to do with her life then sit in this office and watch the years pass by? Maybe she'd take that vacation after all. She had to do something if she were ever to leave this listlessness behind.

She looked up and smiled. "Really, Amelia. I'm fine. Thanks for checking."

"Hmm...you're welcome."

Stephanie turned back to the paper the moment her office door closed. Her heart did a pathetic little rolling thing as she stared at the black and white picture of Nick. He looked a lot different. He still had the same grin, the one that could turn arrogant as quickly as it could turn boyish, and the same piercing eyes. But his face was clean-shaven and a dimple she never knew existed winked at the corner of his smile.

God, he looked good — so virile and male. It was no wonder she'd fallen for him.

Knock it off, dumbass, you're going in the wrong direction!

Stephie was right, though she really had no business intruding on her thoughts at work. Stephanie had opened the newspaper to find a date with a stranger. Nick wasn't a stranger. Not really. She didn't know a ton about him, but she knew the things that mattered. Like he'd only been interested in her for sex. And that he clearly wasn't above making up shallow lies about taking a new job that involved travel in order to make her understand just how much he didn't want to see her again.

So much for the compassionate man of her forbidden memories. He was just another jerk in an endless sea of them. A jerk she loved with all her heart.

Sniffing back her unwanted emotions, she folded the paper closed. Her gaze pulled to the heavy black caption next to Nick's snapshot, as it disappeared out of sight. Was he as good a writer as he was a cook? Or better yet, as he was a lover? What did he even write about, and why hadn't she read his column before? Maybe she had without realizing it.

It would probably be a wise move to familiarize herself with his work. That way she could best avoid it in the future. More importantly, she could best avoid running into him and making a fool of herself the way she was bound to do.

Stephanie's hands shook as she reopened the paper and sought out Nick's picture. Her heart quickened as she took in his smiling face, then stopped altogether for one frantic second as she read the bold-faced caption beside it.

"No way in hell. This can't be happening," she whispered.

He couldn't really be quitting the paper. That had just been an excuse he'd made up to let her down more gently. But if that were the case, then why was his goodbye spelled out in black and white for the entire city to read?

Ache pressed against her heart, spreading fingers of pain through her body. She bit the inside of her cheek as tears welled in her eyes and a sickening truth settled in her stomach. They were never going to see each other again. No more weekend pleasure cruises. Not even the chance meeting on the street. He was leaving. Forever.

And she was just fine with that.

Okay, so maybe not fine. But she wasn't going to shrivel up and die simply because he'd chosen to pursue a career and a life elsewhere. It wasn't as though she'd believed a weekend of great sex would be enough to keep him around, secretly hoping and praying she'd come to him. She wasn't naive like that. Really, she wasn't.

Oh, damn, who was she kidding? Of course, she was!

No matter how many times she'd tried to forget about Nick, to remind herself all he wanted from her was sex, she hadn't succeeded. She would never succeed because she loved him. And he loved her too. He just hadn't realized it yet, but he would. She'd make him. She'd lure him back to her place, cuff him to her bed and torment him with her tongue if that's what it took to make him see how much she cared. She'd do anything he wanted and more, in order to win him over to her way of thinking. No stake was too high, no risk too great. Not when Nick was on the line.

Starting today, right this second, she was a woman on a mission. She was going to find Mr. Right and make him listen to reason. Make him understand just how much they belonged together. How much more they shared than chemistry. Love might suck at times, but there was no way she'd give up on it without a fight.

* * * * *

Monday morning he'd board a plane for Fiji—an island known for surf, sand and barely clad beauties. Not exactly a rough place for his first travel assignment. So why then did the idea of flying away into the wild blue yonder make Nick's gut churn?

There was an easy answer to that, of course. One with honey blond hair, a killer body, and deep brown eyes a man could get lost in if he wasn't careful. Good thing he'd been careful. He might have fallen for Stephie, but not hard enough that he hadn't been able to get over the affliction. He'd quit thinking about her days ago.

For the most part he had anyway.

He couldn't control those images his brain conjured up when he least expected it. Her dark eyes burning with passion, her pouty red lips parted and beckoning for his own, her breasts bursting free of their itty-bitty confines to fill up his hands, while he filled her slick, wet pussy with the rest of him.

He groaned as his cock began to harden, and shifted uncomfortably in his office chair. He ought to be used to the sensation by now. He spent the better part of his days like this, in a state of semi-arousal. On the bright side of things, now that Stephie wasn't around to tempt him away from food, he was back to a normal eating routine. Blue balls couldn't kill a man, but starvation would without a doubt.

A knock sounded on his office door, and Nick cursed. He'd been waiting for his coworkers to finish up for the day to join him in farewell drinks. Didn't it figure they'd show up now, when it looked like he'd pitched a tent in his slacks?

He slowly made his way through the all-but-barren office, mentally calming his erection as he went. A woman's soft muttering drifted to him when he reached the door. *Ah, shit.* Worse than one of the guys finding him this way, he had to contend with one of the gals. With any luck, he could get her to leave.

"I'm just finishing up in here," he called through the door. "I'll be ready to head out in a couple of minutes."

"Nick? I need to talk to you."

Damn. Whoever it was, they weren't going to go away. He looked down and thankfully noted his hard-on was no longer recognizable, then stepped back and pulled open the door. A blonde stood with her back to him, a blonde he was certain didn't work at *The Tribune*. He would've remembered the shapely legs exposed beneath her modest dark brown skirt. Not to mention her scent. A light floral essence that stirred to life the parts of his anatomy he'd only just managed to calm.

"Can I help you?" he asked.

She turned around slowly. Well-formed curves beneath a sleeveless white top came into view first, followed by a pair of full, pouty red lips. Unease stirred through him as he lifted his gaze higher, then turned to all out tension when he met her eyes. Deep brown ones that matched her skirt perfectly.

Sonfoabitch. She'd come to him. Why?

"Stephanie," he said, struggling to keep his tone flat.

She frowned. "Why do you call me that?"

"What?" No way had she'd tracked him down just to ask about her name.

"Why do you call me Stephanie?"

All right, so apparently that *was* her reason for being here.

Nick tried to form an answer, but he couldn't get past her appearance. She looked so different. Her long hair pulled back in some sort of knot-like thing and nary an inch of skin sticking out for his viewing pleasure. All right, the bottom half of her legs were showing and all of her arms, but those weren't the areas he had in mind.

"I guess I thought it was your name," he finally said.

"It is, but I never told you that."

"Oh." He stared at her for several long seconds, waiting for her to say something further. She remained unmoving, her eyes vacant as he could ever remember seeing them. It was damned near impossible to believe this subdued woman was the same one who'd spent a weekend teasing him with her naughty words and naughtier actions.

"Is that why you came here?" he prompted. "To ask about your name?"

She licked her lower lip and shook her head. "No. I, ah, read your column. I saw it was your last day and wanted to wish you good luck."

Damn near impossible to believe she was the same woman, but the way his shaft responded to the lusty swipe of her tongue, guaranteed it most certainly was her. Whatever reason she had for coming here, to discuss her name or something else entirely, she had to go. One more lick and he was liable to do something he'd regret, like pull her into his arms and ravage her right where they stood.

Nick grabbed the doorknob and jiggled it, hoping his intention would be clear. "Thanks for stopping by. I appreciate it. Now, unless you have—"

"So, you're in a hurry?" Unidentifiable emotion entered Stephanie's eyes. She flashed him a teeth-baring smile then glanced past him.

He nodded, not caring for the way she'd looked into his office any more than he cared for the way his insides warmed with her smile. "I'm going out for drinks with some of my coworkers. They should be here any time."

"Oh." Her mouth fell flat and she took a step back. "I won't keep you then."

"I have a few minutes." *Ah, fuck. Why the hell did you go and say that?*

Because he was talking with his cock again, just the way he'd told himself he wouldn't do. Least of all when he was within the vicinity of her, the woman who'd provided him with too many wet dreams the last couple weeks to count.

Stephie's smile returned in full detail, and the warmth in his insides spread, fanning hope he knew better than to harbor. She reached out and touched his arm, pulling back almost immediately but not nearly soon enough for his comfort.

"It's okay if you're too busy, Nick. I just wanted to…"

"Yeah? You wanted to…?"

She glanced past him again, then drew back to his eyes. "I wanted to tell you goodbye," she said softly. "And I did, so I guess I'll see you around."

Without another word, she turned on her heel and started away. Nick's arm shot out and spun her back on its own accord. She stared at him wide-eyed. He was equally astounded by his move. It was bad enough he couldn't keep his penis in check around her, now the rest of his parts seemed to be taking on a mind of their own too.

Well, hell, maybe his hand knew something his brain didn't. There was only one way to find out… "Is that why you really came here, Stephie, to say goodbye?"

She licked her lip again, and he bit back a moan. "Uhmm…yes?"

The hope he knew better than to harbor grew with the uncertainty of her response. He moved his hand from her arm to her face, caressed her sun-kissed cheek. Her breath caught, and he fought a smile. If that wasn't too goddamned ironic. Bad girl Stephie jittery as a schoolgirl and all from a simple touch.

Intrigued by her behavior, he tucked a wayward strand of hair behind her ear. He trailed his fingers along her neck on their journey back to her face, and a barely audible squeak escaped her lips. Her eyes widened farther, and she jerked her gaze away.

Unfortunately for her, she hadn't been quick enough.

In a blinding rush of comprehension, reality hit Nick square between the eyes. This wasn't bad girl Stephie standing before him. It was good girl Stephanie. The woman he'd first guessed her to be when she stepped from her Beemer two weeks before. The one who'd lost control in his arms time and again, even though to do so went against her mantra regarding sex and, at least that first time, secretly terrified her. The one who kissed him with such honesty, such devotion that it stole his breath away.

His Stephanie. The one he loved.

He couldn't hold back his grin as he moved his hand lower and ran his thumb over the lushness of her bottom lip. She drew in a sharp breath, and his grin widened. She'd finally come to her senses and realized just how much they belonged together. Not because they were born to fuck, or whatever other lame ass excuse she preferred to toss his way, but because they loved each other. At least that better be what was going through her head right now, because if it wasn't he'd probably have to kill her.

He caught her chin in his hand and tipped up her face, forcing her to meet his eyes. "Should I take a guess at why you're here, sweetheart?"

She gulped, her pupils contracting. "If you...if you want to."

Hell no, that wasn't what he wanted to do. What he wanted to do was to follow up on his first instinct and ravage her right where they stood, but that would be a bad idea. At least, it would be until he confirmed his suspicions and got her to admit the real reason she'd come here—because she'd missed him just as much as he'd missed her.

"All right, I'll take a stab at it. I think the answer's 'no'. I don't think you came here to tell me goodbye. I think you came here because you realized you missed me and what we shared on the *Hidden Desire*."

Stephanie's eyes narrowed and she shrank from his touch. "This isn't about sex!"

Halla-fucking-lujah! She finally understood. "No, what you and I have isn't about sex. It's about feelings. About how I haven't been able to get you out of my mind since the moment you walked into my life." He heard the breath catch in her throat and brought his hand back to her cheek. "It just about killed me to watch you walk away, sweetheart. But I knew I had to let you go, that it's what you wanted."

Her eyes flew wide and she recoiled. Stephie emerged before his eyes, her grin scathing and her hands fisted at her sides. "What *I* wanted?" she shrieked. "You've got to be kidding me. *You're* the one who wanted to keep things between us purely sexual. You acted like you were going to keel over the second the word love was brought up. I might add, by your own big, fat, lying mouth."

Nick dragged his hand through his hair, his temper growing nearly as fast as his confusion. "The only one acting on that boat was you, sweetheart. Acting like you gave a damn about me, when deep down all you wanted was someone to fuck.

"'I'm sorry, Nick,'" he mocked, "'you're a great guy, but I'm just not in the market for a relationship. I just want sex from you. Lots and lots of it.'" Okay, he'd made that last part up, but too damned bad, she deserved it. "Oh, and let's not forget my personal favorite. 'You and me, Nick, we were meant to be together. We were born to fuck.'"

He snorted at the words. Looking back, they were almost funny. So damned funny it hurt to speak. "The only thing I was acting like, scratch that, pretending like, was that I didn't give a shit you only wanted me for sex. I cared about you, goddamnit, really cared, and all you cared about was getting laid."

He crossed his arms over his chest, his temper flaring ever higher, and waited for Stephie to lash back. But she didn't say a word. She just stood there with her mouth hanging open and her eyes squeezed tightly shut. A sob shook through her, tripping hollowly from her lips. She slapped her hand to her mouth and gaped at him.

Ah, Christ. She was going cry. No, Nick corrected as water trickled down her cheeks, she was already crying. He hadn't meant to make her cry, knew how much she must despise him for pushing her threshold. But, damn it, he'd really needed to get those things out and, hell, she'd started it.

He reached a hand out and rubbed her arm. "Stephanie? Are you all right?"

She shook her head, sniffed. "Oh, Nick, I've made such a mess of things."

His gut knotted at the desolation in her words, the tears that brightened her eyes. This wasn't all her fault. If he'd stuck to his guns, and maintained the nice guy image he'd always prided himself on, none of this ever would've happened. They would've kept to their own cabins and only spoke to one another when she boarded and disembarked the *Hidden Desire*. At the same time if he'd stuck to his guns and ignored her delicious curves, she wouldn't be here now, and he wouldn't be clinging to his hope of a steamy and fun-filled reconciliation on the island of Fiji.

"So things got a little messy. We can fix it, right?" He took her hand and pulled her into his office, closing the door behind them. "Why don't you sit down and tell me what you think you've done that's so awful."

Stephanie glanced at the chair he'd indicated, but remained standing. She sniffed again, then swiped at her cheeks and cleared her throat. "I lied to you, Nick. I lied about a lot of things, and because of it, I hurt us both. I blamed you for everything, for letting me walk away, for how unhappy I've been the last couple weeks. But it wasn't you. None of this was your fault. It was all mine."

"Last thing I knew, it took two to tango, sweetheart." He smiled at her, and she frowned in return. "Regardless of whose fault it was, it's in the past."

Her frown grew bigger and her eyebrows drew together in disbelief. "Didn't you hear me? I lied to you. I'm not even a bad girl, Nick. Do you know when the last time I had sex was before I met you? Do you?"

"Yes."

"Of course you don't, because I made out like I was this— "She stopped short, and gaped at him. "What did you say?"

It was all Nick could do to not pull her into arms and ease the world of guilt clouding her dark eyes. He jammed his hands into his pockets to waylay the temptation. "I said 'yes', I know when the last time was."

She shook her head. "I don't understand. How could you?"

"Because every once in a while you let your guard down, and told the truth. You told me other than that first time, you hadn't had sex when the guy wasn't tied down. Then the next day you told me I fulfilled your fantasy of bondage. I've never confessed to being the sharpest knife in the drawer, but those two things don't add up."

Stephanie gasped, then sniffed, then shook her head again. "I can't believe it. That whole time you knew." She pinned him with a baffled look. "Why didn't you say something? Call me on my lie?"

"You didn't want me to, just like you didn't want me to be in love with you."

Her eyes went wide, and she whispered, "To be in love with me?"

"It wasn't a mistake what I said that day. I just hadn't meant to say it yet. We'd just met and it seemed so soon, but an hour hasn't passed since then, when you haven't been in my thoughts, in my heart. I love you, Stephanie, and I want to be with you."

Fresh tears welled in her eyes and her chin wobbled. "But…but you're leaving."

"Only for a few weeks, and I'd hoped you would come along with me. That is, if you have the time. I know you have a career to think about, friends and a life, but—"

"Yes." She flew against his chest, all but knocking the wind out his lungs, and squeezed him to her. "I want to go with you, Nick. I don't even care where it is."

He freed his hands from his pockets and, wrapping his arms around her, breathed a sigh of relief. *Thank God. They were going to be all right.* "I'm glad to hear it, because I was a little worried about asking how you felt about Antarctica."

For a second her squeeze lessened, then it grew tight again and she smiled up at him. "Antarctica's perfect. We can keep each other warm."

He laughed. "I was joking with you, sweetheart. It's actually Fiji."

"Hmm…even better. We don't have to wear clothes."

She nuzzled against him, her lush breasts rubbing at his chest and shooting fireworks of need straight to his groin. He was never going to get any work done with her along, but, hell, what a good reason to lose a job.

Stephanie rose on tiptoe and brushed a soft kiss over his mouth. Her eyes glistened with unshed tears when she drew back. "I've missed you so bad. And I love you, honey. I don't know what I would've done if I'd lost you."

"Oh, Stephanie…"

"Oh, Ni—"

He stopped her words with his mouth, and kissed her with all the love he'd denied believing in. She kissed him back with fervor, with hungry urgency, her tongue darting out to lick hastily at his lips. He parted his mouth and drew her in, savoring her sweet taste as his hands moved down to cradle the ass that had haunted his dreams and fantasies for way too damned long.

She slid her hand between them and stroked his erection through his slacks, breathed a husky whisper against his lips, "I think someone wants to play."

Nick groaned as she brazenly caught him in her palm and squeezed. "I like your mindset, sweetheart, but the door isn't locked. The guys are bound to be here at any moment, and I doubt they'll knock before entering."

Flashing a mischievous grin, Stephanie moved her other hand between them and unbuttoned his slacks. "Come in and catch us making love?"

He grinned, able to read her thoughts loud and clear. There was a time when the idea of being caught with his pants down would have bothered him. But that was before he'd met Stephanie. "Yeah. Come in and catch us making love on my desk. Of course the way you carry on, they'll probably hear your screams long before that."

Easing his zipper down, she slid her hand into the front of his briefs and freed his bulging anatomy. She cupped him in her hand, and licked her lips, as if in anticipation of doing the same to his erect cock. "And the problem with that is?"

He chuckled and pulled her tighter. She might not be a bad girl by nature, but she was when the mood suited her. And it did suit her, to a glowing perfection.

"You are amazing, Stephanie Lang," he said, lifting her into his arms with the express purpose of delivering her to his desk. His palms brushed over the hem of her skirt and he gave into his urge to see what lay beneath. A fiery red thong revealed itself, and all the blood in his body hammered to his balls. Maybe making it to the desk wasn't important after all. Come to think of it, the floor looked pretty damned good.

"Amazing, huh?" she asked as Nick lowered her to the carpet.

He moved between her bent legs and ran his tongue up her silky thigh until he reached the juncture. "Absolutely stunning," he rasped, pulling her panties aside to gain access to the glistening, pink mound beneath. He rimmed the edge of her swollen sex and watched in awe as her clitoris quivered, puffing up before his eyes.

He flicked his tongue over the nub, grinning when she writhed against him, fisting her hands in his hair and calling out his name.

"Absolutely stunning," he repeated, grabbing hold of her hips and pulling her back to his mouth. "And all mine."

About the author:

Jodi Lynn Copeland resides on 30 acres of recreational woodland and farmland, minutes from Michigan's state capitol. She has been writing since her junior year in college when she began a romantic suspense novel. Since then she has written numerous books, which range from single title mystery to erotic romance, and has won various writing awards. While not writing, she enjoys time in the outdoors—hunting, fishing, playing ball, or just spending time with her family and pets. Weekdays are spent on her day job as a technical writer, graphic designer, and web programmer for a national engineering firm, and evenings and weekends bringing tales of passion, romance, and adventure to life.

Jodi is a member of Romance Writers of America (RWA), Greater Detroit Romance Writers of America (GDRWA), Mid-Michigan Romance Writers of America (MMRWA), Cata-Romance, and a dedicated critique group.

Jodi Lynn Copeland welcomes mail from readers. You can write to her c/o Ellora's Cave Publishing at P.O. Box 787, Hudson, Ohio 44236-0787.

Why an electronic book?

We live in the Information Age—an exciting time in the history of human civilization in which technology rules supreme and continues to progress in leaps and bounds every minute of every hour of every day. For a multitude of reasons, more and more avid literary fans are opting to purchase e-books instead of paperbacks. The question to those not yet initiated to the world of electronic reading is simply: *why?*

1. *Price.* An electronic title at Ellora's Cave Publishing runs anywhere from 40-75% less than the cover price of the <u>exact same title</u> in paperback format. Why? Cold mathematics. It is less expensive to publish an e-book than it is to publish a paperback, so the savings are passed along to the consumer.

2. *Space.* Running out of room to house your paperback books? That is one worry you will never have with electronic novels. For a low one-time cost, you can purchase a handheld computer designed specifically for e-reading purposes. Many e-readers are larger than the average handheld, giving you plenty of screen room. Better yet, hundreds of titles can be stored within your new library—a single microchip. (Please note that Ellora's Cave does not endorse any specific brands. You can check our website at www.ellorascave.com for customer recommendations we make available to new consumers.)

3. *Mobility.* Because your new library now consists of only a microchip, your entire cache of books can be taken with you wherever you go.

4. *Personal preferences are accounted for.* Are the words you are currently reading too small? Too large? Too...ANNOYING? Paperback books cannot be modified according to personal preferences, but e-books can.

5. *Innovation.* The way you read a book is not the only advancement the Information Age has gifted the literary community with. There is also the factor of what you can read. Ellora's Cave Publishing will be introducing a new line of interactive titles that are available in e-book format only.

6. *Instant gratification.* Is it the middle of the night and all the bookstores are closed? Are you tired of waiting days—sometimes weeks—for online and offline bookstores to ship the novels you bought? Ellora's Cave Publishing sells instantaneous downloads 24 hours a day, 7 days a week, 365 days a year. Our e-book delivery system is 100% automated, meaning your order is filled as soon as you pay for it.

Those are a few of the top reasons why electronic novels are displacing paperbacks for many an avid reader. As always, Ellora's Cave Publishing welcomes your questions and comments. We invite you to email us at service@ellorascave.com or write to us directly at: P.O. Box 787, Hudson, Ohio 44236-0787.